KAI Tortured

New York Mafia Vengeance:
Book 3

Alexandra Iff

"And in the end, we were all just humans, drunk on the idea that love, only love, could heal our brokenness." — F. Scott Fitzgerald

Contents

CHAPTER 1

ORION

"What the fuck are we gonna do with her now?" I slam my fist on the wooden table. "Fucking Maisy, she knew this. She must have. She can't tell us she has a photographic memory and knows nothing about this. We *know* she knew. Do we agree?"

I stare at Logan and Kai, who are sitting in front of me in my kitchen. The bottle of whiskey and three empty glasses are on the table. I'm asking, no, begging them to agree with me. For once, I'm right. In fact, all this time I was right. *Fucking Maisy.*

The revelation that Maisy is Goran Slavinovich's daughter tears me apart. All of this is a meticulously planned betrayal. *It must be!*

But they just look at me. They're hurt, I feel it, and no words they say would make them feel better. She hurt them. Hurt us.

It would have been easy if it was anyone else – I'd just slice their throat open and cut their limbs off – but Maisy?

Kai shakes his head. Logan's eye twitches sporadically. It's involuntary, he is dealing with either hate or anger, but when he remembers who he is thinking about, it stops. He's fighting monsters inside him.

Kai's totally and utterly defeated. I doubt he's thinking of the Slavs. Maisy's on his mind, and the fact that she's off limits now.

Dirty. Fucking. Slav.

There it is. *Off limits.* An enemy.

Cleverly inserted between our lines to divide us and annihilate us. And she's been doing a pretty good job so far.

"To think we went to Riyadh to save her," Logan mutters.

"We're not doing this. You hear me? We're not gonna wallow in the fucking Slavs' lies. She lied to us. We were gullible, and that's that. End of. We move on. Usually we kill them, but her... Fuck, I don't even know what we should do with her."

Kai speaks up. "We don't kill her. She had so many chances to kill us, but she didn't. We'll give her that much."

"She must've known she's a Slav, Kai," Logan reminds him. We can't plead ignorance anymore. Or even hope that she hasn't lied to us, about everything.

"What evidence do you have? Her sister's word?" *Kai's actually defending her?!* "We don't know Rosey, and on top of that, she's spent the last ten years with Milan. Come *on!*"

I'm so furious I can't think straight. "Evidence? I'm sure we have evidence. She's been lying to us every time she opens her mouth!"

"A fucking Slav," Kai mutters despite himself, rubbing his hands over his face.

The curveball she threw caught us off-guard. None of us know how to deal with it.

"A fucking Slav," Logan echoes sadly.

"Why do I still want to fuck her?" I ask, standing up. "Shall we?"

I don't know what made me say that. I'm mad enough to want to hurt her, but this? Raping her? That would be a step too far. Although not unheard of. Goddamn. The world I'm hoping to build is not made for people like me right now. People who want to harm out of vengeance and spite.

Kai and Logan raise their eyes to me at the same time. Their brows furrow. I know what they're thinking. But I'm angry. I need this anger dealt with.

Kai stands and squares up to me. "You touch one hair on her head, and you'll have me to deal with."

"Since when have you become such an asshole?" Logan snaps.

His disgust tells me I went too far. Their reaction only riles me more.

"What, now you're taking the side of a Slav? A Slav, Kai?" I yell in his face. "A Slav ordered your father's death, remember? She should be shot. That's the only way our problems will disappear. The *only* way!"

"I swear to God, Orion. You touch her, you die."

Kai's threat lingers in the air.

I throw my hands up and stare at him in disbelief. "You did *not* just say that to me. Tell me you didn't."

Kai's standing his ground. "You heard me."

"What the fuck are you gonna do with the fucking heir to the Slavs?" I thunder. "Everyone will want to kill her when they find out! We prepared for a war on them, then we protect their *leader?* The true heir to the Slavs? Have you lost your mind?"

"Both of you, sit down!" Logan barks at us. "We need to make a plan."

"If it involves killing Maisy, it ain't gonna happen." Kai reaffirms his position and sits his ass down next to Logan. I follow.

"Why are you protecting her so much?" Logan asks Kai.

"As much as I hate the Slavs, and *her* right now, I believe her. She couldn't have known."

"Stupid. You're *stupid*, Kai!" I growl at him.

"Orion, I'm warning you. Next time, I'm gonna swing my fist your way."

"And I'm gonna pull my gun on you, and then what're we gonna do? Tell me! Are we gonna kill each other, and lose everything we have, over a woman? Let alone a Slav? A fucking *Slav*, Kai?!"

Kai and I lock eyes, neither of us willing to secede.

Logan clears his throat. "I'm going to say something now and it won't be easy, but it has to be said," he starts, and pours himself a full glass of whiskey.

We wait until he drinks it in full and looks at us.

"She must be killed."

"No!" Kai slams his fist down, the empty glasses bouncing on the table. He shoots back to his feet. "Maisy's staying alive. You're gonna have to kill me first before you kill her."

I never thought either of them would agree. It's the best option for all of us, clearly, and I want to kill her, but I also don't. I'd rather imprison her than kill her. But then, practicalities. Fuck. There's no way out of this. She's gonna have to die.

"Orion?" Logan is after my support.

My mind is split in half, with one half stronger than the other. The stronger one wants Maisy alive. *What the fuck is happening to me?*

"If it has to be done, then so be it." I'm focused on getting my words right, not to falter, all the while my heart is being surgically removed. I can only imagine how Kai feels. And Logan... These past few weeks were hard on him. Having been roughed up by the Slavs has made him the sanest in this discussion. And maybe the only one who's able to be unemotional and detached. In any case, it's what we need right now.

"I'm going to Maisy's room now." The dark edge to Kai's voice is alarming. "You come near her, either one of you, you die."

He heads toward the stairs. His hands are curled into fists. He's angry, and ready to protect Maisy with his life. That much I can see.

I turn to Logan, but there's a wall in front of him, one that hides all of his emotions. The Slavs took away the once cheerful and relaxed Southerner out of him. He'd never been tortured for that long. And I wonder how long it will last, or if it will ever end. I don't have an ally here right now, nor even a friend. I have another mafia head sitting next to me.

"I'll deal with it," he says, as if he heard my thoughts. "I'll find an assassin. One who'll kill her painlessly. We won't see it, and it'll just feel like she left."

Alarm bells are ringing. He already has a solution in his head, before even discussing it with me. "And Kai?"

"Kai's gonna cry for a few days and then he'll be fine," Logan concludes flatly.

I shake my head. "Logan, as much as I'm with you, you saw him. He's hurting. That's his way of coping. I want to slap some sense into him but right now, we can't do much until the dust settles. Seriously. He'll be like this for a few days, I know him. He'll hate her just as much as we do, but he won't let her die."

"Do *you* want her to die?" Logan asks blankly, catching me off-guard.

I lean back in my seat, my eyes landing on my empty whiskey glass. Before I respond, I fill up the glass and down it. He knows what I want. *But we have no choice.*

"All I can say is that not killing her leaves open a can of worms. Worms that want to take over New York. And with her being alive, our very existence comes into question. If I have to choose between us and her, it's us. It hurts me to say this, but I choose the Cartes, the Delgados, and the Vitalis over Maisy."

Logan's hard stare mellows. "Fuck, man. I know how you feel."

It looks like I've managed to reach Logan's humanity, if only for a moment. "Yeah." I pick up the bottle of whiskey and refill our glasses. In silence, we drink all of it.

"I'm gonna head home," Logan says.

"Sure."

"The sooner I get rid of her scent, the better," he mutters. "She's in my head constantly. Thinking about killing her causes me real pain."

"Then don't think. I can deal with it," I offer, although it'll be the hardest thing I will ever have to do. If it means he doesn't have to suffer, I will gladly take that on. As the oldest of the three of us, I should take responsibility for having trusted Maisy in the first place and allowing her to move into my house. *And into our lives.*

"No." His voice hardens again. "I'll do it."

He stands up and, without delay, leaves the kitchen. I hear the front door slamming as he exits.

I don't waste any more time down there. I head upstairs, straight to my bedroom, avoiding Maisy's room. Kai's there anyway, and he'll kill me if I approach. I'll let him have his hero moment. He always does this, then realizes he's being a hothead and succumbs to whatever we agree. Although tonight, he's extremely agitated, and it may take him longer.

As I approach my bedroom, and I'm finally alone with my thoughts, the gnawing in my chest intensifies. Maisy is a Slav. She's just like us. Head of a mafia clan. Considering they've wanted to take over New York for years, this is the perfect opportunity for the Slavs. If they're using Rosey for breeding, they'd use Maisy for that, too. My blood boils when I think of that, and all my instincts are telling me is *Protect her*, but then, they'll never give up. They'll never stop. They'll find her eventually, and she'll bear God knows how many of Goran Slavinovich's heirs. The life she'd be living would be one of torment. If she dies, she'll be better off. But we'd also figuratively die with her. Either way, we lose. A life not worth fucking living. And here I am, talking to everyone about a better future.

Our families will definitely have a better future, with Maisy gone. But not us.

LOGAN

"It's Logan Vitali," I answer upon hearing a cold "Yes" in reply to my call.

Lukash Bussetta, a recluse belonging to the Vitali cartel, is famous for his success. Why? Because he never misses. I know he'll do the job when I tell him to.

A voice devoid of feeling comes through on the speaker. "You got a job for me?"

"Maisy Roy. Or Maisy Slavinovich."

"Maisy Slavinovich?" *That's got his attention.* "Interesting."

"Is that a problem?" Goddamn. I knew her name would raise suspicion, although I'm sure word about Maisy being a Slavinovich has spread by now.

"Not at all. Maisy Slavinovich it is. What's her whereabouts?"

"I don't know." I'll give her this chance, perhaps a moment with Kai. Though the reasons why I'm doing this elude me. Her death is inevitable.

"Consider it done."

The line goes dead and I look at my cell to confirm he's gone. Suddenly, I become aware of a feeling I've never experienced in my life – a weight. A huge weight on my shoulders. I can't shake it off; it just sits there, pushing me into the ground.

It's either us or her.

And I'll be damned if it's us. My father worked too hard to leave me his legacy for a girl to take it away. Not on my life. *Fucking Maisy. Fucking Slav.* And yet, I can't move from where I'm standing.

What have I done?

CHAPTER 2

KAI

Fucking assholes. Maisy is our whole world, and they want to kill her? Not on my watch. She's hurting so much right now, and she needs us, that's for sure.

I enter her room quietly and see her lying on the bed, facing the window. She hasn't even bothered to take off her boots. The black dress she wears is crumpled up underneath her, and she looks so small and beautiful and helpless in the large bed.

She's... art. That much I know. If I could freeze-frame this image in front of me, I would. Because no matter what I do, or how heroic I act, I know soon it'll be over.

My baby girl is the ugly hell of the Slavs, incarnate.

But I will never believe that she knew. I know my Maisy. I'd have seen the signs, for sure.

Do I want her to turn around right now, and run into my arms? Fuck no. I'd push her away.

Still, stupidly, here I am standing. By her side. I've never taken a girl's side before, and always followed Orion's or Logan's guidance. They seem to have more brain cells than me. Clearly, not this time.

I promised her the day she came into our lives that I would protect her, and here I am. Keeping my promise. I just didn't know I'd have to protect her from the people I know and love.

I sit my ass on the chair opposite the bed and wait. I know she heard me come in. I hear her whimpers. She's been crying all this time for sure.

Slowly, she rolls over on the bed to face me. She clasps her hands together under her cheek, her knees bent and pulled up toward her chest. She's curled up like a snail. Her eyes, bloodshot red, look straight at me. "What are you doing here? You might get cooties from me."

That makes the corner of my mouth crook up. Why does she have to be sassy right now? Unintentional for sure. While we were planning her demise, she's been torn apart, crying, knowing perfectly well what we have in store for her.

I straighten my face quickly. "Don't talk to me." I don't want her to think I'm her friend. Because I'm not.

Because eventually, I must go back to Logan's plan. Fuck. *What was I thinking, coming up here?*

"Huh. I should've known. You're here to keep an eye on me."

I *am* keeping an eye on her. But to save her, not to kill her. I want to tell her that I believe her, but I can't. She must know she's a prisoner right now.

I stand up, turn on my heel and stride out quickly, rushing almost. Straight downstairs and back toward the kitchen. *I made a mistake.* This is harder than I thought. When Orion and Logan see me, they'll know my bravado was as pointless as everything else in my life. I bet Orion knew that all along. They may even be laughing about me right now.

I enter the kitchen and immediately reach for the whiskey, which I desperately need a bottle of right now, vaguely aware of my surroundings. I was expecting to see Orion and Logan but they're gone, and Martin's here instead. He's sitting comfortably in Logan's spot, holding his glass on the table. Lucky for him, he hasn't taken mine.

I take the bottle and fill my glass, then top up Martin's too. I pick it up in silence, clink his glass, and down it in one.

"Thanks, Kai." Martin lifts his glass and drinks. I bet he doesn't know what transpired in here twenty minutes ago.

"Did you take Milan to the Slavs?" I ask.

"I did. I emptied a round in his body when we dumped him in the front yard. All good in here?"

"Yes... Yes." The idea forms in my head instantaneously, out of nowhere. "Say, d'you think you could loan me your ride for tonight?"

"My ride?" Martin's eyebrows shoot up in surprise. I'm not sure if he doesn't want to part ways with his car, or if he's thinking ahead and cannot believe his luck.

"I'm taking Maisy out," I say matter-of-factly. "I don't wanna take her on my bike, it's too cold. Why don't you take it instead? For tonight only. Or until I'm back." I throw him my keys, which he catches. I know he's gonna love the swap. I mean, who wouldn't?

He grins and pulls his own keys from his pocket. "White Dodge Caravan, parked out front. Thanks, man!"

"Sure." Out of everything, this was the last thing I thought I'd ever do. But it is what it is. I must protect her. Here, she's not safe. I'm gonna take her someplace no one can find her.

I take his keys and go up the stairs, not sure if I have the nerve to follow through on my idea. After this, there'll be no going back. Fuck. I don't want that. But I also want Maisy alive. They don't get it. She's the most important person to me. And to them. They just don't know it yet.

"Get up, pack your bags," I order as I re-enter her room. "We're leaving."

"Leaving? Where?" Her gorgeous head lifts, her eyes curious, but not afraid. With me, she's never afraid. I love that. She knows me too well.

"We're leaving this place."

"And Orion and Logan?"

"They're not coming."

"But... they know?" There's a strange trepidation in her voice. I probably have the same feeling, but I'll be damned if I let them kill her. It's exasperating.

"No, they don't, Maisy!" I yell.

"So, you're not gonna... You're not gonna kill me?"

I regard her without saying anything. No one else would know what's going on in my head right now, but she does. She can see the love I have for her even through my hardened exterior. She knows me, and her face lights up infinitesimally.

She just nods to herself, accepting my request. I hate that she knows I'm on her side. I'm not. She's a fucking Slav.

"You're not off the hook yet, Maisy. I'm still not decided on what to do with you."

Maisy doesn't respond. Whatever I say right now, she's seen through me. She just packs her bag with some clothes and puts it over her shoulder. She sticks her free hand in her pocket and pauses, just like a fashion model showing off the latest summer collection. Irresistible. My cock aches for her.

"Ready." She pulls out a scrunched piece of paper from her pocket, takes a moment to read it, then throws it on the bed. "I'm ready now."

"Let's go." If Orion or Logan run into us now, I'm fucked.

Martin is gone from the kitchen, which is a bonus. At the front door, I take Maisy's coat from the hook and help her with it, then put on my leather jacket. As I open the front door, I hear my bike zooming off. Perfect timing. I'm hoping Orion will be looking at the bike and not his front door when we leave.

The white Dodge is parked just outside on the street, and I quickly usher Maisy inside.

This is it. I may have just fucked up the one good thing I had in my life.

MAISY

All this time, I was desperately looking for someone to save me, to protect me from Milan, from the Slavs, and as it turns out, I'm... I'm... I'm a filthy Slav myself.

Goran Slavinovich. My father, apparently. A murderous, sadistic brute. No wonder he gave Milan the green light to do whatever he saw fit with us. My stomach flips, making me nauseous. That lecherous cockroach of an asshole, instead of using our brains, resorted to the most heinous, backward thing in the world. Breeding us, to grow the Slavinovich bloodline.

How do I come back from that? Can I at all? My men, the only men I ever trusted in my life, the men who put their lives on the line for me, who saved me so many times, now hate my existence with a vengeance.

What have I done to deserve this life, to be thrown about like a piñata, everyone taking shots at it? Not being able to decide my own life constricts my breathing.

Life without Orion, Logan, and Kai would be... not worth living.

And if I'm taken back to the Slavs, they'll tie me to a fucking breeding bench and fuck me until I get pregnant. That would be my life, on repeat, every nine months.

I'd rather die.

At least when I die, this pathetic joke of a life that I'm living, where I'm used and abused, will stop.

But Kai taking me with him, away from Orion's house, could mean many things. I'm confused. Is he feeling sorry for me? Will he set me free in the wilderness that is New York, like I'm an animal? Even I know that my chances are slim to none if he does that. The Slavs are everywhere. No, he's probably taking me back to them. Not wanting to have blood on his hands, pretending he's saving me, but really, he knows full well what fate awaits me. With Milan dead, Rosey's position is set as the leader of the Slavs. Although, how can they see her as a leader if she's just fucked to bear children, without free will?

I'd rather die. The mantra pounds in my head like a hammer.

I'd rather die.

I hear Kai's voice behind me. "We'll go in here."

Having parked in an alleyway and urged me out of the car, he's now guiding me to a door at the rear of a tall building. The sign above reads *STAFF ENTRANCE.*

He keys in a code and the door unlocks. He seems to know his way around the place as after walking me through the pitch-black corridor, he ushers me through another door. The moment it opens, it's clear by the blaring sound coming from inside that it's a movie theater with a showing in progress. The large screen lights up the room, and I see there are a few people in the audience.

In the darkness, we walk up the stairs to the last row where he gestures for me to sit down. I do, and he takes the seat next to me. I'm not sure he planned all this because I notice him exhaling the breath he was holding, as if I'm a burden he's been stuck with.

He leans his head back and stares up at the ceiling.

"K-Kai?" *I am not going back to the Slavs, and Rosey – that vindictive, jealous, cruel sister of mine.*

"Please, Maisy. Not now. Just watch the movie."

The big screen in front of me has a foreign film showing, Italian I think. I don't understand a word they're saying. I try to make sense of it but am distracted when, from the corner of my eye, I see Kai turning his head and watching me.

I wait for a few moments before I decide whether to say anything. I turn his way and meet his gaze. He's staring at me with so much angst in his eyes, it hurts just to look at him. I want to scream at him that I never chose my blood. I want to make him believe me, but right now, we're just staring at each other in the darkness, his face illuminated on and off by the movie playing on the screen.

"I'm not strong enough to resist you, Maisy." He sounds like he's in agony.

But I know Kai; he understands me. I shorten the distance between us and press my lips to his, and right at that moment, I feel as if this kiss is going to deliver us from all the sins we've committed, charging the air around us with love and understanding.

I pull back, searching for his eyes, but they're closed.

"Please, don't stop," he murmurs.

It's as if he's not allowed to take control of the kiss, because then… then, he'd be kissing a Slav. Let the Slav take advantage of him. But his words are the fuel I need, and I don't care as long as I get to kiss his lips.

The kiss feeds my craving for him, and I don't hold back; gradually, it becomes hungry and passionate, and I pull away again. I want him to see the certainty in my eyes. I want to show him who I am. Maisy Roy. The girl he promised to protect, no one else.

"I said, don't stop…" he breathes.

My hands are on his chest, and I scrunch his t-shirt in my fists as I pull him closer. This is it, there's no going back. My body is awake and responds like that of a tigress. I want him, right here and now. My hands roam all over his body and down to his bulge. It's dark in here, and in the theater seats we're a little constricted, but I manage to hook my leg over his knee and he reciprocates by sliding his hand up my thigh, taking the hem of my dress with it.

I throw a glance down at the men sitting in the few rows below, some turning away from the movie to check us out.

"Don't worry about it." Kai takes hold of my jaw and pulls me back to his lips while his hand on my thigh journeys higher, his thumb stroking me under the dress, coaxing me to open my legs.

"Baby girl, you do something to me," he whispers in my ear as he kisses my neck. "Fuck me if I know what that is."

He reaches as high as my waist, hooks his fingers in my panties, and proceeds to take them off. I help by lifting my bottom and pulling them down, and his hand goes back between my legs while mine returns to rubbing his bulge. I didn't think he'd ever touch me like this again.

I know he's still battling his demons, but he's squeezing my inner thigh and then going straight for my nub and as he makes contact, I stifle a moan. I give in, and open my legs wider. My hips slowly begin to roll into his fingers, swaying back and forth. His thumb is firmly pressing my clit as I lift my foot onto the seat in front, giving him space for maneuver. I cover my mouth with my hand, trying to suppress my moans as I slide down in the chair.

But that's not enough for him. He stops everything he's doing, slips out of his leather jacket, then gives me a quick kiss on the lips before kneeling down, between my legs.

"Kai... people are watching," I manage to whisper before he starts eating my soaked cunt. My throbbing clit is being sucked, hungrily, as if this is the first time he's ever done it. He grazes my folds with his teeth, and I can't help but think he wants me and hates me at the same time. My hips sway with his tongue, asking for more, and my body is screaming as I stifle my moans, biting my lip while I tightly grip the armrests.

The way he's ravaging me, it feels as if I've been denying him my cunt all this time. He spreads my folds and exposes my clit again, and it's like thunder strikes from heaven when his tongue flicks across it, bringing bursts of explosions, but only small ones. The biggest one is building in the background and, with his fingers inside me, thrusting knuckle-deep, I'm flying. But this is for him, not me, although I'm close, almost there, and when he comes up and plays with my nipples through my dress, tugging at them with his mouth, I can't hold off any longer. I try to hump his hand, arching my back, wanting more when his lips attack my neck. His fingers jerk harder inside me and my eruption hits.

"Kai!"

I'm flying high to heaven, trying oh-so-hard to be quiet, but some of the people in here are watching us, I'm sure. I cover my mouth again but it's futile, my suppressed staccato groans escaping as I start convulsing over him, like a pyroclastic flow nobody can stop, ripples of my orgasm spreading through my body while he tries to still me.

I cup the back of his head and pull him to me. His lips brush over mine, and he bites my lower lip. At the sting of pain, I pull back. Only then do I hear a derisive noise from a few rows below.

The movie is finished. I'm certain everyone heard me.

"Sorry." Kai rests his forehead on mine for a brief moment. "Wait here." He stands up and fixes himself hurriedly. His cock has been strenuously distended in his jeans, but he's keeping it in, it seems. He pulls out his gun from the back of his waistband and walks away from our seats.

What is he going to do? "Kai?"

He scans the theater, taking in all the faces around him. Five men were apparently watching our show, and are still staring at me from the middle rows. That's where Kai's heading.

He walks in between the rows to get to them and within moments is standing face-to-face with the men, who smirk disdainfully at him.

But as Kai walks under a spotlight and his face is illuminated, they freeze. They recognize him. Without saying a word, Kai points his gun and shoots the first one in the forehead. The shot echoes around the theater as he slumps in his seat, and the rest of the men leap up and run for their lives. But even I know it's in vain. Kai aims, and one by one, shoots all of them as the rest of the people in the theater scream and run for the exit. They're all dead within a minute.

Looking satisfied with what he's done, he comes back up to me.

I don't condone killing, but fuck me if that was not hot. *Is this a sign of the Slav blood running through my veins?* Well, those fuckers *were* looking at me the whole time.

"Now, where were we?" Kai smirks.

I shoot up onto my tiptoes, run my fingers through his hair, press my lips to his, and remind him exactly where we were. I'm the last person who would resort to killing, but his power makes me drunk. My hands roam over his jeans where they strain over the bulge. I unbutton them and pull his cock out, pumping him a few times before I decide what I'm going to do. I choose to get on my knees.

"Fuck, Maisy, you know what I need."

I lick the precum off his cock and don't wait to take him fully in my mouth. And it's as if this is what he was waiting for all along, he weaves his fingers into my hair and slowly pushes my head down on him, checking to see how deep he can go. When I can't take him any more, the gagging sound I make makes him stop, and instead he pulls me back and bobs my head, each time pushing deep into my throat, to that sweet spot just before I choke.

"Yeees, that's right, baby girl."

I suck, twisting my tongue around his glans as his veins pop in my mouth. His cock is getting rock hard and he's picking up speed, but the waves of pleasure are crashing on my shore, too. He pulls me up by my hair, my spit leaving a silky trail from his cock to my lips. Both of us are panting heavily.

"Kai," I breathe.

Roused like an animal, he kisses me deep before he turns me around, my back to his front, and sits down. He shimmies my dress back up to my hips and pulls me down to sit on him. His hard cock is just about to slide into me as I look back at him, and I hold him there, at my entrance.

"You want me, Kai?"

He groans the moment my cunt touches his glans, and he hands me the reins. I impale myself on him and start riding him, tilting my behind as high as I can because… fuck, it's in his face and because it feels fucking awesome! Right now, fucking is the only option for my sanity. It's how I know he needs me.

I rotate my hips sideways, rubbing myself on him, his low growls driving me crazy. My insides are racked with pleasure as I fully surrender to the dance, but after a while, he's had enough of playing. His hands suddenly grab my hips and he starts pounding me hard against him, primal grunts escaping his mouth, leaving me to receive my dose of ecstasy through his violent thrusts, just as he starts ejecting his seed into me.

"Mmhhmmm!" His hands wrap around my body, holding me still while he empties every last drop inside of me.

CHAPTER 3

ORION

This feeling I have is unsettling. After the short shut-eye I had this morning, I woke up with a surreal feeling that all this is just not happening. That we can't have fallen out over a girl.

I also woke up with a hard cock, painfully reminding me that there is one person inside this house that I should never, ever fuck again. Because she's a fucking Slav.

I'm glad Kai got his sense of reason back. I heard his motorbike last night but by the time I got to the window, he was gone. I only saw him in the distance as he drove off. Still, he came to his senses. I knew he would. He wouldn't allow a girl to come between us, although if I'm honest, this time, he really connected with Maisy.

After Natasha, we didn't think he'd come back. Natasha killed his father and nearly got Maisy gangbanged, and Kai still didn't think she deserved to be killed. He gave her a pass. God knows how many passes he would have given her if Maisy didn't decide to shoot her. Fuck. That was fucking unreal. Maisy knows how to use a gun. That also riles me up. She has so much information but she chooses to share only what she wants. There's so much that we don't know about her.

Coffee. That's what I need. Coffee.

I get up, buck naked with my cock swinging left and right, and struggle to contain it inside my boxers. I don't bother getting dressed – I know Lisa won't be coming and it's only Maisy and me here. Martin and Phil's jobs ended when they got rid of Milan's body last night. They're probably gonna come back, but they'll stick around outside.

And if by any chance I run into Maisy, well, so be it. Will I fuck her? I want to. I probably will.

Fucking Slav. I bang my fist against the door of my bedroom before stomping out and heading downstairs.

I won't. I won't fuck a Slav.

You've been fucking a Slav all this time. And loving it.

I throw a glance at Maisy's room, just in case the door's open. I really wish she'd had the guts to leave this morning. Maybe try to escape. That would have been great, because then I'd know what to do with her. Right at this moment, I'm stuck. When I'm alone with her, I either hate her or fucking crave her. And even when I hate her, I still crave her in a strange, insatiable way.

Once in the kitchen I keep myself busy, adding coffee grounds to the filter, then the water, and wait for it to brew. Leaning on the kitchen counter, I look around. Huh. I fucked her a few times in here.

Fuck! Evoking memories is for pussies.

I quickly turn to the coffeepot and pour the first few drops into my cup. I'm running out of patience with everything.

As I take my first sip, my eyes land on the far end of the kitchen counter, where the package I received yesterday is sitting. The package from Marina.

I stare at it for a few moments. Or maybe longer. My mind is so riled up over what has happened that I'm not sure I want to deal with this right now. But on the other hand...

Marina was really something. If only we had more people like her. I asked her for a favor and she did it, no questions asked. As if she was a Carte. And I know she actioned it instantly because she was taken by Milan that same night, when she left Kai's house in Long Island.

I walk to the end of the kitchen counter and pick it up, double-checking the label – it says *Dr. Marina Connely*, and the name of the hospital she worked at.

I never thought I'd have an answer this fast. My PI has been fucking slow coming back to me with my requests. Either he's dead or… Well, he better be dead. *Fucking asshole!*

In a way, I want to savor the moment before I open the package. Fuck knows what I'll discover when I do, but it seems lately all I'm predestined to receive is shocking news.

I take a knife from the cutlery drawer and slide it over the opening, slicing the label and making a cut in the box. I don't know why I'm adding so much significance to this. Actually, I do know why, but what I'm hoping for is ridiculous and I'm doing this only to confirm my ideas are absurd.

I open the flaps of the box and inside, I see a single letter.

Am I excited? I check myself. I've got no emotions, because it's a far-fetched idea Maisy has been feeding us for nearly a year, and it's just that, far-fetched. Yet even I started to believe her lies.

I skim through the letter quickly, but as I do, I find myself going back to the same few lines, over and over.

The percentage of the genetic match determines your sibling status.

Your genetic match is 25%, which is sufficient confirmation that you three are half-siblings.

I sit down at the table with the letter still in my hand.

"...you three are half-siblings."

How the fuck is that possible? I'm trying to figure out how on earth one woman slept with Willer Carte, Mickey Delgado, and Lorenzo Vitali. Gave birth to three sons, and none of them knew about it.

I have brothers. Fuck. *Is this real?* This changes everything.

I'm still in shock when the sound of Kai's motorbike shakes me from my daze. He's come back. I left my cell in my bedroom, but I'm sure the security cameras would have pinged if it was necessary. Even so, I wouldn't have bothered looking at it. I have men outside, and I know it's him.

Do I just tell him? Do I prepare him for this? How will he react? And Logan? Half-brothers...*fuck.* We're brothers. This can't be real. We'll have to do another test to confirm.

Did Kai have any idea what was inside when he saw the package from Marina?

I get up and hurry to fill my cup with coffee. I want to stand in wait for him when he walks in. It's funny; I'm nervous for the first time ever. I ought to be mad at him for how he left last night, after threatening us. And now, I don't know how to act. A million thoughts swirl in my head, and I start to go over each of them.

I've been alone in here for quite some time. I realize he's not coming in.

My cup is empty, so I pour myself a refill and head out.

It's strange for Kai to stay outside but then again, he may be talking to Martin and Phil. We did say we need to be friendly.

I leave the letter on the kitchen counter and head to the front door. I open it slowly, wanting to see what's going on without startling anyone. Another reason I'm nervous is that I'll be talking to Kai for the first time as his 'big' brother.

When I pull the door fully open I see only Martin and Phil, talking in low voices. They're wearing their winter coats, in contrast to me in my boxers.

"Oh, hey, boss." Martin looks oddly excited, a huge grin plastered on his face.

I look beyond them. I see Kai's bike, but not Kai. I nod at Phil. "Where did he go?"

"Who?" Both of them seem confused.

Goddamn stupid men. "Kai. Where did he go?"

"Oh, that." Martin grins. "You mean, his bike?"

Phil pipes up. "He's not here, boss. He swapped with Martin last night. He was just telling me about it."

I'm hearing what they're saying, but a sense of déjà vu overwhelms me, though I reject it. I reject it because I remember not checking my cell when Maisy went to Logan's club. And I also remember everything that happened afterward. My whole mind just shuts down and yet, I'm standing in front of my house, with a coffee cup in my hand.

Kai, my newfound little brother, is finally gonna get the beating he missed out on all these years.

Martin seems to pick up that something's wrong. "Boss?"

"He has your car?" I ask, as calmly as I can. Although at this point, I sense my nostrils flaring in anger.

"Um, yeah. He wanted to take Maisy out and didn't want to take her on his bike. It was cold. Aren't *you* cold?"

He's suddenly worried for my well-being?

"He has *Maisy??*" I thunder. That's it. I can't be calm anymore. I sense the steam coming out of my ears. "Talk, Martin. *Was—Maisy—with—him?*"

"Yes, boss." Martin knows me, and he knows how close to dying he is. "I'm sorry, boss. He asked me, and I-I thought we were okay with the Delgados. I let him have my car. Sorry, boss. I-I'm sor—"

"I need your registration! Text it to me!" I shout and slam the door in his face.

"Arghhhhh!" I growl on my way up to the attic, where my laptop is, where I need to figure out where Kai went. I suddenly have enough anger to shift the world off its axis.

On the way up, I stop at Maisy's room, just in case. To see if Kai really did what he did. I walk inside and check the ensuite. *Fucking Kai!* Her closet's open, and some of her clothes are missing.

On the bed is a scrunched-up piece of paper, probably some whining apology of a letter. I disregard it and race to my bedroom where I pick up my cell, then continue to the attic.

I dial Logan's number first. I must tell him what Kai's done, but it goes straight to voicemail.

"Call me as soon as you hear this message!" I bark into the phone.

Then, I call Kai. *Kai, you better answer me, you fucker!*

His cell also redirects to voicemail. "Kai, you don't know what you've done. Call me as soon as you get this message!"

Fucking idiot! Every living person in New York will be after her, and they'll kill anyone in their way.

LOGAN

Everything is wrong. *Everything.* Even waking up this morning in my penthouse, at the top of the world, doesn't feel right. My world collapsed the moment I found out Maisy was a Slav. No wonder she wanted to kill Milan. She didn't want him to tell me about my mother. And for that, I can never forgive her.

But was hiring Lukash too much?

The *fuck* it was. But then again, she shouldn't die at the hands of some random person. If she's dying, *we* should kill her. I'll just point the gun at her and look away. That's how I killed my first Slav, anyway. This shouldn't be any different.

Fuck! Fuck! Fuck!

I can't believe I put a hit on her. I grab my cell from the bedside table; I have a missed call from Orion. *Shit! Has she been killed already, and Orion's informing me of the fact?*

I call Lukash, but it just rings. Why did I think he'd answer? The moment I ordered that hit, I knew there were no takebacks. It's a done deal. The hit is as real as the daylight.

I dial Orion's number next. I've never been as worried in my life as I am right at this very moment.

"Logan!" The distress in Orion's voice is real.

Goddamn! "Is it done? Is Maisy dead? Has she been killed already? Tell me!"

"What are you talking about? No! Kai has her!" Orion roars. "The fucker took her last night without telling anyone!"

"What? And those two idiots at your house – why did they let him go? For fuck's sake, Orion. Kai's in deeper shit than he knows."

"Yeah, tell me about it. I'm gonna kill that motherfucker when I get my hands on him."

"No, no, you don't get it. Orion, last night, I called a hit on Maisy. I was in a really bad place, and Maisy... she killed Milan. And with her being a Slav, I thought there was another reason why she killed him and, I got angry."

"You *what?!*" He's furious, and rightly so. "Logan, you...you... Call it off! *Now!*"

"I can't reach him, goddamnit! One way or another, it will be done. He's thorough."

"Shit! You just had to do that, you fucker! Where are you now?"

We must think, and make a plan, as we always do. "I'll get to yours as fast as I can."

"No. Meet me at the Delgados'."

"He won't be there, Orion."

"I know. But we gotta inform them. The war over Maisy's still raging."

"Sure. I'll meet you there." I look at my cell to cut the call but I hear him still talking. "What? Did you say something?"

"Yeah. There's one more thing."

"What?"

Orion's silence is strange, and fucking unnerving. *More bad news?* "Orion, what?!"

"I opened the package from Marina this morning."

"Why? What was in it?"

"That day in Long Island, when I saw her to the car, I asked her to compare our DNA. As a doctor, she could easily get access to our files."

As I lie naked on my bed, a sudden feeling of adrenaline is injected into my blood, overwhelming me. My heart races, a wild drumbeat echoing the chaos of my emotions. Instantly, I sit up.

"Logan." Orion's voice is now calm. Too calm. "Are you ready?"

For this piece of information, I was born ready. Except I'm speechless and afraid of what'll come out of his mouth.

"The three of us. We're..." he starts, and I already know what he's gonna say.

I stop him. "We can't be. We *cannot* be. This is some kind of Slav ploy, and Marina was in on it. Come on, Orion, don't tell me you're this gullible?"

"We're half-brothers, Logan." The words are clear. And they're here. In my ear.

"I don't believe it. I don't. There's no way. Someone would've known. Someone *should've* known…" I'm on the verge of spiraling, but he brings me back.

"Logan. Stop it. It took me a while to digest the news myself. We're brothers, man." I hear him chuckling. "After all this time, against all odds… we're brothers. Imagine that. And one of you, I want to kick the shit out of right now. If that's not a brother, I don't know what is."

"No. It's too easy." Still, I reject it. I've been looking for my mother all my life, yet my family, my *brothers*, have been with me all this time?

"The evidence is here in front of me."

"Well, if that's the case, I may have just killed my brother. Thank you for that."

"You haven't. We'll find a solution. We always do."

"Fucking idiot, taking off on his own," I mutter, angry that not only have I handed Maisy a death sentence, but I've endangered Kai's life, too.

"How soon can you meet me at the Delgados'?" Orion asks.

I check my watch. "Fifteen minutes."

"See you there."

Orion cuts the line, and I'm left with so many questions in my head, although they ought to wait until we find that idiot who took Maisy.

I shoot to my feet and start dressing. My black three-piece suit is clean and freshly pressed and as I'm preparing it, the realization sinks in. Sweet Jesus mama. My mama was Orion's mama and Kai's mama. I look at the mirror, at myself. It can't be. And yet, as I put on my boxers, I try to think of similarities between our bodies.

None of us look like each other. *Lies. These are Slav lies.*

It can't be this easy.

Today, I'm gonna kill as many Slavs as possible. *Fucking Slavs!*

If Maisy comes out of this alive, I'm fucking her straight into her grave. She's caused me so much stress, and shaved at least twenty years off my life. *Fucking Maisy!*

"Uncle Jon!" I yell through the door. Uncle Jon is always close by. He's a God-sent man, or father-sent, and always looks after me. But surely he must have known something about my mother. I did ask him once, but he didn't have an answer, and the subject was closed and has been ever since.

"Yes?" Uncle Jon enters my bedroom.

"We have a situation. The war with the Slavs is starting and we need everyone ready and prepared. Not sure where it's gonna be, but what I do know is that they're still after Maisy and will try to get her one way or another. Our goal is to keep her alive. Right now, she's with Kai, we don't know where." Saying Kai's name for the first time since I found out we're blood-related gives it a different sound, somehow.

"Logan..." he starts, hesitantly.

I button up my shirt and look at him, waiting on him to continue.

"Everyone's been talking about her this morning. Apparently, she's a daughter of Goran Slavinovich."

I tuck my shirt into my pants. "And your point is?"

He looks exasperated. "My point is that the Slavs will want her back."

I stop and stare at him coldly. "Did you not hear me when I said there is a war with the Slavs?"

"Is the war about her? Or something else?" Uncle Jon asks. "Are we using her to get to them, or are we protecting her? You gotta be clear, Logan. People will make up their own minds if the order isn't clear enough."

"For fuck's sake, Uncle Jon! It's complicated! Just make sure my men are ready to kill every Slav who approaches." I add my favorite piece to the ensemble, the blades in my pockets. I then grab my jacket and turn to him as I leave. "Except Maisy. She's to be kept alive." I remember, and stop for a moment. "And Kai. Keep Kai alive too."

I leave Uncle Jon shaking his head at me and enter the elevator. A woman. A fucking *woman* will be the death of me. Of us. My father died because of a woman; I will die because of a woman. A fucking stupid man, I am.

42

CHAPTER 4

ORION

From the outside, the Delgados' bar exudes ferocity and rebellion. It's daytime, and still there is a glow of a neon sign flickering above the front door.

The few bikers outside, all decked out with weather-beaten leather jackets and metal emblems, are keeping watch.

I'm standing on the sidewalk, completely out of place in my smart three-piece suit, observing the new windows they got after our most recent altercation. Last time I was here I wore a balaclava, and I saved Maisy from getting gangbanged. And now, again, it's because of Maisy that I'm here. *Fucking Maisy.*

I shake off the feeling of frustration and throw a glance at Emilio, my driver, parked on the road. Another car pulls up, a cab, that gets my attention. It's Logan.

He pays the driver and climbs out, joining me on the sidewalk.

Standing across from him, I wonder if the innate pull I feel with him is because we're related. Like the one I feel with Lisa. He doesn't have siblings, and didn't really have a normal childhood, hence he wouldn't necessarily recognize it. I love him, I've loved him as a brother since before finding out what I now know, and it doesn't change my emotions. Except now I know I'm fucking vulnerable to the core.

Logan looks at me, and hesitantly, as though he's battling the idea of having a brother, he opens his arms. This is my brother in front of me. I still can't believe it.

He grins and shakes his head. "It's fucking crazy, right?" he mumbles as I embrace him.

My brother. It's surreal. "Crazy or not, it's real."

"How certain are you? Because when all this turns out to be a big joke, I'll be the first to say I told ya so! Come on, Orion, we knew our fathers well. There wouldn't be a chance in hell that they'd allow for this to happen. Right?"

I shrug, having no answer for maybe the first time in my life. I'm going to allow this. Kai and Logan are like brothers to me anyway, so nothing has really changed. In fact, I like having them as brothers because I'll have more of a say in their safety.

"Let's find Kai. How about that?" I snort, although if I'm honest, I'm really worried for Kai.

Logan nods. "Yeah, yeah, let's get the little prick."

I open the door of the bar and hold it for Logan. At the same time, I look around – it's embedded in me, to always be on alert. "Let's get inside."

Logan enters, and I quickly follow right behind him. "I'm waiting on someone to track Kai's cell location," I tell him quietly.

The Delgados' bar is a raucous place, with laughter and clinking glasses ringing throughout, but even with all that noise, the moment they see us, a fidgeting silence ensues. That's a good sign, because in a similar situation in the past, we'd have been killed on the spot. This is progress.

I make our intentions clear. "We're looking for Kai."

I get nothing back from any of them. They look at us without saying a word, and their hands hover close to their firearms.

"Have you heard from him?" Logan asks.

A sturdy man, leaning confidently against the bar, pipes up in a very deep voice. "We haven't."

Clad in a weathered leather jacket and tattoos that form a tapestry over his wrinkly skin, he seems to calm everyone in the bar with his presence.

"And you are?" I ask him.

"The oldest Delgado you'll find around here," he says. "Tom."

The bartender pours him a shot of something clear. Without taking his eyes off us, he downs it and slams the glass back down on the bar.

As if on cue, my cell pings and I check to see if it's the news I'm expecting. Sure enough, my police contact finally sent me Kai's cell location.

"Right. If he comes here, tell him we gotta talk to him. It's imperative that he calls either Logan or me. Got it?" I nod at Logan to signal that our time here is finished.

Tom, who appears to be in charge, nods, then gestures to the others to go back to how they were. We head out as the hubbub in the bar resumes.

My cell pings again, this time it's a message from Martin.

'Kai wants me to bring his bike to the Hilton Garden Inn. Thought you'd wanted to know.'

Damn right I do!

Logan and I make a beeline for my car. "He's taken her to a hotel," I announce. "Get in." I open the door for Logan and jump in after him. I then show him the message from Martin. "He's asking for his bike. I'll get Martin to keep him busy long enough for us to take Maisy back."

"Good plan." Logan agrees.

Emilio glances at me through the rearview mirror. "Take us to the Hilton Garden Inn, near Battery Park, Emilio."

"Sure, boss."

I text Martin back and read the message out loud as I do.

'Keep him occupied, and away from the main entrance for as long as you can.'

A ping back comes almost instantly. *'Will do. He's at the parking lot behind the hotel. Waiting for me.'*

"We need to find out if Maisy's at the hotel, and which room she's in." Logan's ready for action.

"You'll be sweet-talking the receptionist, while I'll keep watch in case Kai shows up."

Emilio navigates the bustling streets of Manhattan and soon, we arrive at the hotel. "We're here, boss." He pulls over outside the entrance.

"Stay close, and be ready to go." I pat Emilio on the shoulder and climb out of the car. Logan follows me.

There are plenty of people in the reception area, so I manage to get to the elevators without drawing any attention. I look like a guest so it's no problem unless someone recognizes me.

I check on Logan; he's already talking to the receptionist, touching her elbow and being Logan, the sweet-talking, charming Southerner that he is. She bats her eyelashes, blushing, and proceeds to give him a room key. That looked easy. Logan kisses her cheek and bows to her, then heads in my direction.

"Second floor," he mouths.

"She's alone?"

"No one else has been in there." He shows me the key. "Room 2034."

I feel the tension rise as we wait for the elevator door to open. When it does, we enter and I press the button for the second floor, exchanging a quick, silent glance with Logan, one that no doubt speaks volumes about my nerves.

The door slides open on the second floor and we move cautiously along the hallway, trying to be as stealthy as possible.

Both of us are alert, ears straining for any sound that might indicate someone's presence or any hint of trouble. I lead the way, my hand lightly resting on the handle of my Colt.

Once we reach room 2034, we pause outside the door, looking at each other and exchanging a final nod of readiness. I place a finger to my lips and carefully slide the card into the slot, hoping to trigger the mechanism quietly. We hold our breath, waiting to see if we'll be able to enter without drawing any attention.

The moment the light on the lock turns green, we enter the room like cats. We see her lying on the bed, with her back to us. By protocol, we clear every corner of the apartment first before we both turn to the bed. She must be sleeping because she doesn't react to us at all.

We don't move, just watch her. It's like being under a spell. How come she can do this to me, to us? I always wondered what sort of power she has to make my cock twitch and ache for her every time I'm in her vicinity.

She's still in the same dress as last night, lying on her side, her legs bent at the knees, her eyes shut. She's wearing her sneakers on her feet instead of her boots from last night.

"Psst, Maisy," Logan says softly.

He's already forgotten what she put us through. *Fucking Slavs.* They ruined everything. And Maisy, she's so... Why does the word 'innocent' come to mind? *Argh. I'm so stupid.*

I nudge her shoulder harshly with the butt of my gun. "Wake up."

Her eyelids flutter open, and upon seeing us, she gasps in shock.

"Logan! Orion!" She sits up, terrified, pleading. "I-I didn't want to leave, I'm so sorry..."

Logan touches her gently, like he doesn't want to startle her. "Come on, you're coming with us."

"And Kai? He'll be here any minute."

Kai is a hothead that I don't need right now. If Logan's hitman tries anything, Logan and I have it covered. We're taking Maisy to my house, and will get our families to protect us. Kai has too much of a short fuse for this kind of protection right at this moment.

"We can't wait for him." I look at Logan. "We don't know what his intentions are."

"You're right. If Maisy's with us, he'll come to us," Logan agrees.

"Correct."

I grab Maisy by the upper arm and push her in front of me toward the door. I want to be anything but gentle, or soft, because the mere fact that I'm touching her thaws my anger toward her.

She whimpers as she walks and I'm quick to loosen my grip. I don't want to hurt her. True, I wish I could kill her, but I definitely don't want to hurt her.

"Why are you taking me away? Are you gonna kill me?"

There isn't panic in her voice, but boldness. I should put her across my knee and spank her ass until it's red.

"We should've done that a long time ago. Now, there's no point," I retort.

Kai's location still shows him behind the hotel, so we leave the same way we came in. Martin is doing a good job of keeping him busy.

We move quickly but carefully out of the hotel, making sure not to attract too much attention. Maisy is between us; we keep close to her, one of us on either side, guiding her through the hallway toward the exit.

The air feels tense as we reach the main doors. I glance outside, spotting Emilio already waiting by the car, engine humming.

As we approach, he catches my eye, giving a subtle nod to confirm he's ready to go as soon as we're all in. Logan opens the rear door while I help Maisy inside, making sure she's seated. I slip into the seat beside her, and Logan closes the door with a soft thud.

"Let's go."

Emilio promptly pulls away from the curb.

"Kai will be mad," Logan mutters.

"Don't worry about it. What did he think was gonna happen after our conversation last night?"

"So you *were* gonna kill me," Maisy gasps. Quietly, she starts to sob.

I don't react. I don't want to argue with her. She's smarter, and she'll see through me immediately. And I can't afford to let Logan see me yielding to a woman.

I'm so fucked.

LOGAN

By the time we get to Orion's house, Maisy's eyes are red and she's sniffling, her cheeks glistening with tears. Her hair's stuck to her face and she seems to have lost the will to look composed.

We walk her up to her room, Maisy first, then Orion, with me bringing up the rear.

"Go and wash up," Orion orders her.

She doesn't speak or react. Right now, she's just following orders.

"Is your house secure?" I ask Orion as she goes into the ensuite.

Orion's texting on his cell, and once he's done, he looks up at me. "Yeah. At least, I fucking hope so. I told the Cartes to keep guard outside. Ten people, changing every two hours."

I pull out my cell and start messaging Uncle Jon. *'Send men to Orion's house. I need people guarding his place.'*

When I finish, I see Orion's made himself comfortable on the chair opposite Maisy's bed while I remain standing, leaning on the wall next to him.

"Are we gonna ask her about us?" I ask quietly.

"Not tonight. She's been through a lot." He rakes his fingers through his hair. "*Fuck!* She's a Slav, but I want her like she's the last woman on earth. I want to fuck her brains out and not stop. Am I losing my mind, Logan?"

"Not as much as I am. Look, *we* make the rules, and we can do what we want. We can either let her go, kill her, or keep her prisoner permanently."

Maisy comes out just then, wrapped in a towel, and catches the end of our conversation. "Keep me prisoner, permanently?" she whispers anxiously. "Or kill me?"

We stare at her without a word as she trudges from her ensuite to the closet. She defiantly tosses her towel into a crumpled heap on the floor and stands before her closet, her gaze lingering over the choices, as if the selection of her panties and skimpy top is the one decision she can control. Deliberately, she sifts through her panties and takes her time, her breasts bobbing around as she moves, her sweet shaved pussy looking perfect for the taking. Is this a quiet rebellion against us, or an act of seduction?

I'm fully under her spell, speechless and immovable. This woman does all that by just being in the same room as me.

Finally, she chooses the 'right' top and panties, dresses, and gets into bed. Just like that.

I'm drunk on her already, not daring to blink as she covers herself with the sheet, then slowly, very slowly, bares her leg and looks at us innocently. She's fucking playing with us, because now she's scrunched the sheet between her legs. What I wouldn't give to be that sheet right now.

"I'm still me," she breathes.

"Mm-hmm." Orion rests his chin on his hand, watching her silently.

She signs out loud and turns her back to us, revealing her round, perky ass poking out of her panties.

Fuck. Either I fuck her or get on with making a plan to protect her. But Orion's pensive look is challenging to understand. We're teetering on the brink of danger, yet here he is, preoccupied by what to do with Maisy.

It's too late now; the moment I attempted to cancel the assassination, it was obvious the tables had turned.

"What's the plan, Orion?" I ask, because being with her is driving me nuts.

"We wait," Orion responds, not taking his eyes off the prize. He has the same thoughts as I do, except he's better at keeping himself under control.

We wait.

I've had enough of standing, and so, despite everything inside me screaming not to, I take off my suit jacket and drape it neatly over the chair Orion's sitting on, walk over to the bed, and lie on my back next to her.

I'm expecting Orion to warn me, to ask me to move away from her, but he doesn't say anything.

And Maisy, she takes my hand and slides it across her waist. My arm is twisted in an awkward way, so naturally, my next move is to turn to her and scoot closer. And spoon her. And I do so gladly.

"Hold me, Logan," she breathes, and sniffles. "Never let me go."

She wiggles her ass into my crotch and the first thing I do is question her behavior. *Is this what life is going to be now? Questioning everything she does? Fuck that.*

I pull her closer and grind myself against her. That sweet pussy is all I want, but Orion's watching me. I usually wouldn't mind but I'm expecting he'll have something to say to me. Although, I bet he wants her too.

"Let you go? Not even in your dreams, sweetheart." I kiss her shoulder, then the back of her neck, and a short, sweet moan escapes her lips. I thought I'd never hear that sound again in my life.

She tries to turn around to face me but I keep her in place.

"Logan, please..."

I pull her closer and slide her on top of my body, making her lie down over me with her back pressed to my front. I want Orion to see her, her need, her innocence. Because I trust her. She didn't know about being a Slav, but also, I know right now that my cock is doing my thinking for me. That's why I need Orion.

I slide my hand under the waistband of her panties and immediately, her head slots into the crook of my shoulder as she spreads her legs on either side of my body, giving me access. My other hand goes under her top and straight to her breasts, squeezing her nipples.

The moment I reach her sweet, hot cunt, I voice my approval with a low growl. She whimpers at my touch and her hot and wanton body writhes over mine.

This is all I ever wanted in my life, and what do I do? Hire a hitman to kill her. My agonizing need for her pokes into her back, but I can wait; right now, I want to play with her. I want my sweetheart. I want my Maisy. I run my fingers across her silkiness, sliding them gently from her cunt up to her clit, where I linger, making slow, round movements as she shivers in pleasure.

She's so beautiful. Feeling her over me is what I needed. I go back down to her honeypot and insert my middle and ring fingers inside her. I glide them out and smear her arousal all over her nub, and her hips immediately start their gyrating dance over me. The waves of pleasure she experiences feel like heaven on top of me. I push my fingers inside her again, feeling the heat of her cunt squeezing me, and lift my head to admire her body while she humps my fingers. Pure bliss.

"*Fuck.*"

I sense movement and hear Orion's hiss at the same time. I'd forgotten about him.

"Look at her, Orion. Her body is…" I pump my fingers inside her as her moans fill the room. "…made for us."

If Orion's hooded eyes could tell a story, it would be a short one. Most likely, a pornographic one. He undresses as he watches Maisy writhing on top of me.

"Logan. Fuck everything. She's ours."

I chuckle at his irritation as my fingers continue their game of sloppy thrusts while with my other hand, I'm rubbing Maisy's swollen clit.

She arches her back, my cue to change my focus, so I tug her nipples hard, one and then the other, until she moans at me that it's too much.

She's trembling on top of me as I finger her, my hand on her clit, rubbing determinedly, while I pinch her nipples beyond her pain threshold. She's thrusting her hips back and forth against my fingers, focused on her eruption, building up unstoppably fast.

"Logan!"

When her explosion arrives, she whimpers in ecstasy, jerking over me, ripples of pleasure vibrating through her body and into mine.

MAISY

Logan's hold, together with the gentle touch of his lips on my shoulder, anchors me, despite the tremors that run through my body. I feel another set of lips tracing a path from my shoulder down my arm, compelling me to open my eyes.

When I do, I meet Orion's gaze. Immersed in the depth of his dark eyes, I'm spellbound as he moves down my body to position himself between my legs. His pecs and six-pack bear tattoos that are too familiar and look so delicious on him. I see the bullet wounds too, a memory of all that's happened. Wearing only his boxer shorts, he gently caresses my inner thighs, and upon reaching my panties, he carefully hooks his fingers under the waistband and slides them off me in a deliberately slow motion.

I'm exposed and vulnerable, yet I feel distinctively different because this is me, my true self, my essence. He didn't accept me before. I'm a fucking Slav. And yet, now, here he is. Hungry.

My breasts rise and fall with each erratic breath as Logan continues to play with my nipples under my cami. I'm losing myself again in the throbbing sensation, and now that Orion's about to do what I think he is, I tilt my pelvis slightly forward.

Orion's hands stroke my inner thighs, and the moment his tongue glides over my pussy, it's pure heaven. I bite my lip to stifle a moan, or a cry, I'm not sure, as my emotions are too intense right now. I thought I lost them for good, and they... they came back to me.

"You like this, Maisy? The two of us playing with you?" Logan whispers in my ear.

"Mmm, yes... *Yes!* Please... Yes."

As Logan holds my body still over this, I whimper and wait while Orion pulls back, then heightens the suspense by blowing on me, ever so gently. I'm ready for the taking, but it feels like slow, excruciating torture. Then it happens; his lips are on my folds, tenderly pulling, gently spreading them wide. The delicious rumble of approval that follows propels me to new heights entirely. I didn't know such heights existed, but I only hit them because I fully let go. I tilt my head back and put my hands in Orion's hair, guiding his energetic tongue.

"O-Ryon!" I'm flying on a magic carpet ride. "I need you, O-Ryon."

"How much do you need me?" he whispers.

"As much ... As much as the fire needs oxygen."

"Fuck Maisy, I'm already destroyed by your fire." Orion's lips descend on me and devour my pussy as I buck on top of Logan's body, whose hard cock has been painfully prodding into my back all this time. I reach beneath me and start unbuttoning his pants. It's time to set him free.

The moment I finish undoing the buttons, it pops out in all its glory. Orion helps me sit up and I straddle Logan reverse-cowgirl, taking his cock and sliding it inside my pussy, both of us groaning from the feeling. I glance over my shoulder at Logan and smile, and he gives my buttock a playful slap.

"Ride me, sweetheart, like your life depends on it."

He chuckles as I start riding, wanton, properly, not cutting any corners, in to the base, out to the tip.

In front of me, Orion pulls his hard cock out of his boxer shorts. It's glistening with precum and his pierced glans calls to me as I grip him with both hands, stroking along the length, remembering how his girth feels when he's ramming inside me. Running my thumb over the glans, I smear the precum, but just before I can lower my head, Orion takes my jaw in his hand and pulls me to his lips.

"I hate you for not leaving my head for a mere moment, ever since I met you."

I lunge at his mouth, grabbing his head with both hands and diving for his lips; I weave my tongue with his and kiss him deeper and harder than ever. He responds with a muffled groan, mirroring my tongue's thrusts. I'm riding Logan as Orion and I violently kiss and gasp for air, our teeth clashing. I think I can taste blood, but it only makes me hungrier.

Riding Logan's cock and rubbing myself off on him, I breed debauchery, surrendering completely to my inner beast as I am willingly torn between my men. The moment I have enough of Orion's kiss, I pull back and go down to take his cock in my mouth. Without prompt, I start with the same hunger, bobbing my head wildly as I ride Logan, my moans betraying me because of the heavenly feeling that overwhelms me.

Logan's hands land on my hips. He's close to losing control as he begins to pound me against him in a frenzy, primal grunts escaping his lips as he does. I latch myself firmly onto Orion and suck him for dear life. I'm gonna show him what life with Maisy Roy will be like for him. All he has to do is choose me.

But it's Logan who helps me close in on my summit, and I'm propelled into wild rotations of my hips, chasing my orgasm.

"Fuuuuck!" His hands grip my hips as he empties every single drop of cum he has inside me, and I cum with Orion's cock still in my mouth, throat-deep.

I try to pull away for air, but Orion is having none of it. Hurtling toward his own ecstasy, his fingers tangle in my hair, gripping me tightly, and I can't move anymore. With him controlling my head, he sets his own pace, fucking my mouth hard, with louder grunts each time, thrusting me against his groin. His rock-hard cock is swelling in my mouth and one last time, he rams and then stills inside of me with a deafening groan while his juices, his life, stream deep into my throat.

"Fuck Maisy, your throat is gold!"

~

It's dark outside and my room is just as dim, except for the glow of a street lamp that seeps through the window, casting a soft light across the bed.

Logan and Orion have me snug between them. Logan is still clothed, except for his crotch, and Orion is naked bar his boxer shorts. We fell asleep just after our make-up session. I'm choosing to call it that. Because why would they have sex with a Slav they despised? And why would they both be holding onto me now for dear life?

"I'm dying for a pee," I say, nudging Orion aside so I can get up. I'm still wearing my cami, but I have no idea where my panties have gone.

Without a word, he shifts over, giving me space to pass.

I make my way to the bathroom and glance through the window when a strange shadow draws my eye. It darts to conceal itself. The whole thing is odd, so I'm left wondering if I actually saw someone from up here or if I'm just half-asleep. I try to focus on whatever it was, and notice Orion watching me.

"Orion, I think I saw some–"

Orion and Logan jump up at the same time, startling me.

"Fuck!" Logan exclaims, quickly buttoning up his pants and tucking his shirt in.

"Get dressed, quick!" Orion orders as he grabs his pants and shirt.

They're scaring me. "What? What's happening?" I run to my closet and seize a fresh pair of panties, a pair of jeans, and a black shirt.

"Put your clothes on, Maisy, quick!"

"I *am!*" I insist, but speed up when I hear commotion downstairs.

There is a sudden eruption of gunfire inside the house, and it sounds like it's getting closer by the second. Shouts and curses intermix with the relentless staccato of gunfire.

Orion and Logan are fully dressed in an instant, Orion with his gun in his hand and Logan, his blades. As for me, I'm being hauled behind them, all of us waiting for whoever's causing this chaos to come running into my room.

After a good five or six minutes, the shooting stops. I try to make out any signs of life from downstairs, and as I do, the door opens slowly. A shadowy figure creeps into my darkened bedroom, likely not realizing we are fully aware of the impending danger.

A man dressed in black, like a ninja, enters with lethal grace, a gun clutched in each of his hands. As he advances, a floorboard creaks under his weight, and somehow, either he realizes he's not alone or he doesn't want to be caught out first, so he shoots into the dark.

With a roar of defiance, but also from being hit, Orion falls to the floor.

"Orion! Orion, are you okay?!" I shriek. I kneel down beside him. The sight of the blood pooling underneath him makes my stomach churn.

"You good, bro?" Logan doesn't wait for an answer. He wields his blades and swings at the stranger, although, because of the dark, he misses.

"Yeah… fucking asshole." Orion is angry most of the time, but injured Orion is exceptionally enraged. "I'm gonna… tear you apart when I get my hands on you… filthy cocksucker!" Despite his fury, it sounds like he's struggling to talk.

Logan stoops down to Orion, and when he sees the blood amassing around his torso, his nostrils flare and his eyes blaze with rage. He picks up Orion's gun.

I sense from both Orion and Logan a fierce determination to protect me at all costs.

But whoever this man is, he's not taken aback by their resistance. He doesn't hesitate for a moment, and his guns both point at Logan. He nods at me. "Let me have her, and I'll let you live."

"You lay one finger… on her… and you're a dead man." Orion sucks in a breath between each word.

"Don't talk, Orion, please," I beg. "You're hurt." He's been hit in the stomach. Or chest. I can't tell where, there's too much blood.

The room has become the scene of a tense standoff, the air thick with the promise of violence. Orion lies on the floor, incapacitated, and Logan stands unyielding, ready to lay down his life to ensure my safety.

The man reaches out to me. "Come on, sweetie, come here."

"Touch her and you die," Logan growls.

"Logan, tell me you didn't change your mind already?"

The intruder knows Logan. I'm confused. "Change your mind about what?" I ask. "What's he talking about, Logan?"

"He didn't tell you, sweetie?" the ninja taunts. "Logan here ordered a hit on your pretty head." His sneering voice makes his words all the more disgusting. "Little did he know that your dear sister paid me a million to bring you to her alive. You have your sister to thank that you're not dead yet."

"You fucking traitor!" Logan hisses through his teeth. "I will personally crucify every living relative of yours before I finish with you."

I gradually rise to my feet and begin to edge away from both Logan and Orion. "L-Logan? You did this? So... So us, tonight, was just... was just..." My voice wavers and I run out of words.

The intruder nods. "Probably one last fuck, sweetie."

"Shut the fuck up!" Orion can barely talk, but still he cuts him off. "Maisy, don't listen to him."

Tears roll down my cheeks as I search for the truth in Logan's eyes, and even though it's dark, it's enough for me to see. "You used me." He's right. It was one last fuck.

The darkness in Logan's expression looks like it's consuming him. "We didn't use you."

"At least be honest. Have the decency to tell me," I whisper, though I'm afraid to hear the bare truth. I tremble as he looks at me. The guilt in his gaze is unmistakable – there's a silent confession right there. My jaw clenches with the bitter taste of betrayal. I see his words on the verge of falling from his lips, each one to cause a heavy blow to my existence. And I wait, expectant, for him to try to somehow bridge the chasm that's deepening between us.

But it never happens. A shot is fired, and Logan drops with a thud.

"Logan!" I scream, and try to run to him, but I'm caught by the man in black.

"Got ya!"

"Let me go, let me go, aaaarrgggggh!" I kick and punch and writhe, to no avail. He has me tight in his clutches.

"I ain't gonna kill you, sweetie, even though Logan paid me to."

"Let her go... Don't you dare touch her," Logan gasps. He's lying next to Orion, a dark, bloody patch growing bigger on his shirt. He's been hit in the stomach.

"Maisy, darling, look at me. Look..." Orion sounds like he's on his last breath.

They were going to kill me, but still, I never wanted them to die. I don't want them to die. They're my... *everything*.

Our eyes meet and it's his abyss that's calming me, taking me deeper, but do I want to go there? With the room in darkness, I may be imagining things.

"Slav or not. We don't care. You're ours..."

I want to believe him, and I wait for more words to come, but there are none. He blacks out. Logan is lying next to him, his eyes closed.

"Noooo! No! Orion! Wake up! Logan!" I sob as the man handcuffs my wrists behind my back.

"There you go, sweetie. See? Easy." The mere sound of his voice is repulsive.

"Let me go. Orion! Logan! No! I won't go to the Slavs!" I cry desperately. "Kill me right now! Kill me, please!"

"Kill you? Of course I won't kill you. I'm not that stupid." He drags me with him while I try to wrench myself free.

CHAPTER 5

MAISY

My head pounds as I try to move, but I'm restrained. *Where am I? What's going on?* My lids are heavy. Everything is distorted and blurry, and dark. I'm lying on a cold floor... in a basement that smells all too familiar. My hands and legs are tied, my mouth taped. I scream through the tape, but nothing comes out but a muffled sound.

"You're finally home, sister."

Foreboding words spoken by someone who should be looking out for me. Only a real lunatic would imprison her own sister.

I can't make Rosey out in the shadows around me. I squint, hoping to get a better look. I pull on my restraints forcefully. I want out of here.

She bursts into hysterical laughter, then grasps my hair with force, yanking my head back. Her laughter is a whisper in my ear. "Oh, the fun they're gonna have with you. You see, I was pliable. But you, you're wild. The Slavs prefer the wild ones."

I haven't felt so much hatred toward a living soul ever. Except for Milan. I'm sick to my stomach. A flashback of Orion's and Logan's dead bodies brings a crushing pain to my chest, and with my chin wobbling, small whimpers come out of me, which turn into sobs when, finally, I give in. Kai won't be able to save me on his own, but I know he'll try. Which means he'll die too.

From now on, this is going to be my life.

No one will be looking for me. I'm as good as dead. And I'd be better off dead.

I hear the heavy metal door of the cell screeching open. Rosey leaves me, three men following her. The key turns in her hand and the sound of the lock resonates in the basement.

"Rosey, please, don't lock me up," I plead, my voice trembling. "I'm your *sister*."

"Why are you locking the door?" one of the men asks her. "Everyone's coming here after dinner."

Paranoia hits me. I don't want to be stuck in here. "Rosey, please! I'll do anything!"

She continues to ignore me. "No one's gonna touch her until we take out her contraceptive implant. Only then will we be certain she can make us babies," she tells the man.

One of the others objects loudly as they walk away. "What? That wasn't the deal! Who cares if she can make babies? Let's test her first."

The door slams behind them.

"Rosey! *Rosey! ROSEY!!!*" I scream into the void, but no one is listening to me anymore. Rosey's gone. "I'll do anything, Rosey! Anything! Just get me out of here!"

~

I wake up to the same stench that's still vivid in my memory. The air is thick with the scent of mold, mingling with the sharp tang of rust from corroded iron bars, which completes the heavy, oppressive atmosphere that makes the basement the last place I want to be in. I'm bloody, bruised, and in pain. And tied up. I never thought she'd go this far. She came back once, and used the opportunity to kick me, use me as a punching bag, and take all her frustration out on me, all while I begged her to let me go. I'm willing to do anything for her to let me go. To make any deal on this earth, just to be free. I've been beaten before, by Milan. But that was different. Milan was not my family.

She is. The powerful and almighty Rosey Slavinovich.

KAI

There's a storm brewing inside me, one that threatens to consume everything in its path. I've been betrayed. Sure, I was the one who betrayed them first, but then why do I feel rage coiled inside me like I'm a viper ready to strike? This has gone too far. It's unforgivable. They played me. I gave Martin my bike, and when I wanted it back, he kept me away from Maisy's hotel room for longer than needed. I never doubted Martin's interest in motorbikes. It just shows I can talk about bikes for hours. And it serves me right for being played. Fuck! I put my bike before Maisy's safety and look where it got her. If she's missing one hair on her head, it would be over for them.

The Delgados and I plan on getting inside Orion's house and taking Maisy with us. And not one person on this earth will stop me.

As I ride, I sense my wrath trying to take over my body. If I squeeze the handles any tighter, I'll break them. My hands crave some action.

It's dark when we arrive outside Orion's house. Four of my men are following me. Actually, one of them is a woman, Zeena, who's very much into mixed martial arts. After Marina, I started trusting women more. I took Zeena with me because she counts for three men when she fights. We are a sight to behold, and also to hear when we approach on our bikes, but I don't care. Let them hear me. I'm taking my Maisy with me, and this time, I won't hide.

I park and nod at the others to park too, and to be ready. I'm expecting some action at any moment now, but nothing's happening. It's oddly quiet.

All of us have drawn our guns. They should have come out by now. I know something's wrong. Especially when I notice Orion's front door is slightly ajar.

I fix my gun in my jeans and run to it.

"Kai, this could be a trap!" Zeena shouts.

Too late; I'm already on the doorstep.

I push the door open, but it's stuck. Something's jamming it from the inside. I peek through and am met with the thick, metallic scent of blood, and see three dead bodies lying on the floor.

"Fuck!" I ram the door harder and step inside. "Get over here, quickly!"

I was hoping to encounter Orion and Logan defending Maisy. I was meaning to kick their asses, too. But the silence here is nauseating, laden with the weight of the unknown.

"Orion! *ORION! LOGAN!*" I run into the living room, where I come across more bodies. Martin's one of them, fucking serves him right for playing me. But his death doesn't satisfy me. He was supposed to protect

Orion. And Maisy, if she was here. Dread runs through me and I race up the stairs, heading straight for Maisy's room. For once, I'm actually scared of what I might find in there… Maisy, lying on the floor, her eyes open, her body frozen… dead… I'm scared that whoever wanted to kill her, succeeded.

But then another thought forms, one I dare not create words for, so I just run and jump over more bodies with a sense of foreboding that clings to me like a second skin. I run until I enter Maisy's room and, the sight I'm met with will haunt me forever. There, sprawled on the wooden floor, are Orion and Logan, their bodies lifeless.

The silence is so profound it's suffocating. My heart plummets into an abyss, and a silent howl is caught in my throat. Guilt. That's what lashes at me instantly. My actions, my decisions, did this. I left them exposed. Unprepared. Had I stayed, none of this would have happened.

What am I going to say to their families? Worse still, what am I going to do without them?

As Zeena and the boys come up the stairs, I kneel beside the bodies.

"Orion… Logan… Please tell me you're messing with me." My voice cracks. *Fuck*. I've never cried in my life, but I feel the tears running down my face now.

What a stupid mistake I made. I now see what they were doing. They were protecting me. They sacrificed themselves so I wouldn't get hurt, because I never stood a chance against... this. My burden to carry for the rest of my days, a constant reminder.

"Kai! *KAI!!* What the fuck? Move!" Zeena pushes me out of the way and checks both men for a pulse. "They're not dead, you jackass! But they will be if we don't get help immediately!"

"Fuck!" I wipe my face and stop wallowing in self-pity. I pull my cell out and dial Uncle Jon Vitali. He answers instantly.

"It's Kai Delgado. Logan's been shot. He needs urgent medical care. Orion Carte, too. We need to take them somewhere safe."

Uncle Jon swears down the phone. "Where are you?"

"Orion Carte's house. Bring an ambulance. Hurry!"

I cut the call and dial Uncle Colletti. Thank fuck we exchanged the numbers of our firsts-in-line when we were planning the war with the Slavs. "It's Kai Delgado. There're twenty bodies in Orion's house. Maybe more. You need a cleanup crew."

"And Orion?" he asks gravely.

"We're waiting for an ambulance. He and Logan have been shot."

"Who did it?"

"The Slavs, most likely."

"Thanks for letting me know." Uncle Colletti rules by vengeance, and is seeing the impact of the Slavs for the first time: twenty bodies, all on his turf. I'm sure the cops will show up soon.

Not even ten minutes have passed when I hear voices coming up the stairs.

"Fucking assholes, the Slavs are asking for it," Uncle Jon swears as he enters Maisy's room. There is another man with him, plus four others dressed in white, doctors, I presume, carrying medical bags on their shoulders and two stretchers. "Quickly, get to them," Jon orders.

My nerves are shot as they hurry to Orion and Logan. They immediately divide into two pairs and start resuscitating them, checking their vitals and whatever else doctors do. If Marina was alive, she'd save them for sure. But she too was killed by the Slavs. *Fucking Slavs.*

"I got a heartbeat. A weak one, but it's there!" one doctor exclaims, and adds supplemental oxygen through a mask on Orion. "We need to get him to a hospital!"

"Thank fuck!" I exclaim, and exhale the breath I was holding.

"This one needs to be in a hospital in the next fifteen minutes," the doctor working on Logan reports.

"*This one??*" I grab him by the lapels of his coat. "*This one* is *the* Logan Vitali, one of the most ruthless mob bosses in New York! And if he heard you–"

"I'm sorry, I'm so sorry, I didn't know. Please, let me take him," he begs. "He really needs the hospital, or he won't make it."

I let go of him, and now Uncle Jon screams at them. "You're still here? Get on with it, come on! Hurry! Get 'em to the hospital!"

Zeena places her hand on my shoulder. "Don't worry, Kai. They'll come back, angrier and more brutal than ever."

"Yeah, they will. I've had enough of the Slavs now. It's time to end this," I mutter, more to myself than to her. I let the doctors carry out Logan and Orion. Trying not to look at the pool of blood where they lay, I jump over it and follow them downstairs.

Uncle Colletti's there already with the cleanup crew, ordering them around.

He looks at Orion as he's brought through and threatens the two doctors carrying his stretcher. "He better survive this, 'cause if he doesn't, I'm gonna find you, and your families, and I'm gonna cut your throats. You hear me?"

I pat Uncle Colletti on the shoulder and follow the stretchers to the front door.

"I'll meet you at the hospital," I tell Uncle Jon, although I'm not sure if I'm gonna go there at all. Logan and Orion are like my family and facing them would mean facing up to what I've done.

Uncle Jon just nods and watches from the door as they are taken into the ambulance waiting outside. He enters too, and they head off with the sirens blaring.

I go back inside the house and walk straight into the kitchen. There'll be whiskey in there. Right now, that's what I need.

I know I look like shit. I'm disheveled, with blood on my hands, my jeans, and my t-shirt. I was enraged when I got here. I was going to take Maisy back, and teach them a lesson, but now I'm realizing too late that I was in the wrong.

This was done by the Slavs. And they have taken Maisy with them.

I pour myself a full glass of whiskey and knock it back, downing the entire glass in one swift gulp. I slam it on the kitchen counter, and right then, my eyes land on a letter. The package from Marina is next to it, opened. The headed paper of the letter has the same logo as the package. It's from Marina. *Fuck this!*

I scrunch up the paper and throw it in the trash before I leave Orion's house.

"I'm out of here!" I yell, loud enough for Uncle Colletti to hear me.

CHAPTER 6

KAI

For the last two months, I have been lost in guilt, remorse, and pain. The night I found them lying in their own blood plays like a loop in my head, torturing me relentlessly.

The bitter irony is not lost on me; I went against Logan and Orion, and now I have no one.

My fears regarding Maisy were confirmed. She's been taken by the Slavs. To my informant, it didn't look as if she was being treated bad. Who knows? Maybe she's been in on all this. I just cannot grasp everything that's been happening because I'm busy crucifying myself every moment of my existence.

Walking the path of despair is not fun. Could I have altered the course of events, had I been there? The question haunts me every day, and there's no escaping it.

Even now, when I know Orion and Logan have pulled through, I'm ashamed to go and see them. They called, they asked for me. Messaged me. Sent men for me. But I'm a big pussy. I'm wallowing in remorse. I lost her, and I almost lost them. They're better off by themselves. I'm just an unpredictable variable in their equation...in anyone's equation. A joke. They're better off without me.

And Maisy, she's a blade in my already bleeding heart. The Slavs want to breed her, and I'm powerless to help her. They haven't started yet, though; they're waiting for something, but fuck knows what. And I know my stupid ass will ride my bike straight into the Slavs' nest, expecting to save her, any day now. That will probably be the day I die. And I'm okay with that. I made my peace with it. I'm okay with dying.

While cooped up in my Long Island house, alone, I've been rejecting every visitor that comes. Not that I've had many. Zeena checks up on me from time to time, and I know she never rides alone; a few Delgados follow her everywhere.

She's been here three times this week, each time bringing news on the Slavs. She's been talking a lot about

Logan and Orion, too. I just ignore it, because what will I do with that information?

I know they're getting better. I know they're staying at Logan's penthouse. Orion has even given his house to Uncle Colletti to use as their headquarters, just like his father did. He's given up on the house ever being secure. Or at least until the Slavs are gone. I bet he feels guilty about what happened. In his head, it's because of him that they got hurt and Maisy got taken.

Today is one of those days when Zeena visits. She's standing in front of me with a pity in her eyes I've learned to ignore. *I don't fucking care.*

"I got a direct order," Zeena starts.

I'm sitting and staring through the window, out to sea. My beard has grown and it fucking itches. I alleviate the itch with my can of beer, which I spill a little as I take a sip. A disgusting slob, that's what I've become. I can't stand myself.

"Who from? Your boss is right here," I say, calm as the sea outside. April is coming, the sun is out more often, and everything is in full bloom. Except me. I'm dying inside.

"Last time I checked, the three families were working together and my direct orders from my boss, i.e. you, were to listen to the Cartes and Vitalis too."

"*Pfft*," I scoff.

"My direct order is to get your ass over to the Vitali penthouse. They've had enough of your wallowing. And frankly, so have I."

"I'd like to see you try." I finish the can of beer, crush it, and throw it at the trash in the corner that is overflowing with many more.

"You think I can't?"

It sounds like she's been waiting for this moment for the past two months, and I turn to look at her. She's intense, resolute, and takes shit from no one. But can she take me? Who knows. I'd like to think my fists are more effective than her martial arts mumbo jumbo.

"Tell you what, I'll let you shave first," she adds.

"Haha, you're funny," I smirk, but in an instant, the chair is pulled from under me and I fall to the floor with a thud. "What the *fuck*, Zeena?!"

My coccyx feels like it almost broke. And that's a fucking terrible injury to have.

"I ain't taking any more of your shit, Kai. Just watch me take your ass to the Vitali penthouse in the next half hour."

She takes a step toward me, maybe thinking I'll flinch, but of course, I don't. I never do, but what I realize is that I'm drunk in the middle of the day, on the floor, and miserable. And I'm definitely not capable of standing up to Zeena. I'd probably hit her if I tried, but in my state, she'd win for sure.

I stumble to my feet. "I don't wanna fight you. Because, you know, I'd win," I slur.

She snorts. "You cocky asshole. Your men need you to lead them, and here you are, afraid and alone, crying yourself to sleep."

"Hey! I'm not afraid!" I point a finger at her. "I'm *never* afraid!"

"Then what is it? Why are you cooped up in here? What made you sink this low and avoid everyone? A girl?"

"Never mind why."

"This has the Natasha stench all over it. Like back when you spent a year letting guilt eat you up."

"This has nothing to do with Natasha."

"I know. This time it's Maisy. Kai, do something. Amend the mistakes you made. Don't just roll over and die."

I study Zeena. She seems to know a lot about me, but then again, every Delgado does. I'm just the asshole who's emotional, crazy, and never owns up to the shit he gets up to. I'm sick of that Kai.

Sighing, I look around me. She's right. I might as well curl up and die. This place has become my own personal pigsty. It reeks, too.

But going back would mean facing Orion and Logan, and I'm not sure I'm ready for that.

"Orion and Logan need you," she says, like she was reading my mind. "Some of the Delgados will only listen to you. It's been too long. They sent me as their last resort. The next thing will be them coming here."

"Fuck." I rub my eyes, stupidly hoping sobriety will kick in. "Give me an hour. Let me shower, shave. Sober up a little. You don't need to wait for me."

She eyes me suspiciously. "You sure?"

"Yeah, Zeena. Thanks. I'll be there by evening."

"Great," she says, but I sense I'm still not off the hook. "I'll be outside. Just in case you change your mind."

CHAPTER 7

ORION

Logan's penthouse overlooks a big chunk of Manhattan, and I find looking at the view calming. In the last few months, this is how I've spent my time. Staring.

Uncle Jon occupies the few sets of rooms down the west side; that's his and Logan's offices, and in a way, the Vitali headquarters. He doesn't come here often and anyway, there's enough space in this damn penthouse for us to never have to run into each other.

Tonight, we're waiting for Kai, and yet again I'm staring out at the city below me. We don't know when he'll show up. We just know that he will.

This day could go either way. Kai's a wild card, especially because we haven't seen him in all this time. I doubt he knows about Logan calling a hit on Maisy, too. He could say or do anything. At the same time, there's so much to talk about, so much to discuss. He still doesn't know we're half-brothers. Fuck. That changes everything.

The day we got shot and were left for dead, Kai was the one who saved us. If he hadn't come, we'd have died for sure. It's ironic; he probably came to kill us for taking Maisy, and instead, he saved our lives. Fate. Huh.

Maisy. A thunder rumbles in my heart each time her name pops up in my head.

That cunt, Lukash, shot us both in the stomach, hoping we'd bleed out. Unlucky for him, we survived, and got our revenge. Uncle Jon got him, cut his balls off, tortured his wife in front of him, then killed her. Apparently the whole ordeal lasted three days. The Cartes decided to contribute to his death, so they cut his fingers off, one by one, then his hands from his wrists, and at the end, his feet. Needless to say, he died in pain. Bled to death.

Our recovery in the hospital has been nothing short of miraculous, a testament to the doctors' resilience and determination. But also, their fear of failing us.

My torso is still wrapped in a bandage, the dressing tight over my wounds. Logan's, too. I glance over at him; I smile a little as I realize that we've been wearing black sweatpants and black t-shirts all this time.

Two whole months of not wearing a suit. It's gotta be some kind of record.

The interphone rings, interrupting my thoughts, and Logan and I make eye contact. He shoots to his feet and strides over to the elevator where the security camera is. I follow close behind.

"It's Kai," he states, and pushes the button to talk into the intercom. "I just opened the elevator doors for you. Press for the top floor when you enter."

Then, he turns to the elevator doors and waits anxiously.

When we nearly died last time, Kai was the one who found us then, too, and who reunited us. Why couldn't he do the same this time? Does he feel guilty that he took Maisy from us? Doesn't he know that had he not shown up, we'd be dead? Or is he still mad at us for wanting to kill her?

The elevator pings, and the doors open to reveal a slouched Kai. Despite his huge torso wrapped in the usual black leather jacket, it doesn't feel as if he's that same guy who'd kill you in a moment with his bare hands. Or that he even wants to be. He's looking at the floor, like he's trying to make himself small. *Goddamnit.* I see it immediately; he's back in that self-loathing stage he was in just before we met Maisy. The regret and self-reproach in his eyes are painful to see.

Guilt is killing him, like a live, palpable entity, but Logan and I will ignore it. We know Kai. That's all there is to it.

Without waiting for him to exit, I'm inside the elevator in a few strides and embracing him. No words. No awkwardness. Just a strong hug for my friend, my brother. Logan is instantly next to me, embracing him too.

At first, Kai freezes. Then, slowly, he lifts his arms and secures his grip on me and Logan. Little does he know that so much has changed since the last time we saw him.

We've been recuperating without Kai by our side for too long, making up excuses as to why he wasn't with us. But I should have guessed. He wasn't mad, just ensnared by a web of guilt and a self-imposed exile. Adrift, trapped in memories that both haunt and sustain him.

"Kai! You fucker!" I finally break the silence and pull back, looking into his eyes, but what I see is unresolved anger, hurt, and love simmering under the surface.

"I'm sorry," he says. "I'm an idiot."

I laugh. "What for? For saving our lives?"

"For... For Maisy. Taking her away when I shouldn't have. If I hadn't done that–"

Logan finishes his sentence. "Then you'd be dead by now. Don't tell me that's the reason you haven't come to see us?"

Kai shrugs and regards Logan, then me. "I fucked up big time. I started a chain of events that led to you nearly dying." He sighs. "And when I saw you lying in a pool of blood..." His eyes gloss over and he wraps one arm tightly around me and the other around Logan. "I wouldn't have been able to live with myself had something happened to you."

I smirk. "It'd take a lot more bullets to kill us, right? Come on, let's get inside. We got a lot to talk about."

Logan's arm is over Kai's shoulder as they follow me to the couch. "Those Slavs signed their death warrants a long time ago," Kai mutters.

"Actually, it was a Vitali hitman gone rogue that shot at us," Logan admits uncomfortably.

Kai stops and turns to him. "A Vitali??"

"In the heat of the moment, I... I hired him to kill Maisy. That's why it was important we find you. He was gonna kill anyone in his way."

"Wait, you hired an assassin, even though I specifically told you not to hurt Maisy?" Kai's fingers curl into fists as he learns this new information.

"I knew I made a mistake the moment I gave her name, Kai. But it was too late." Logan has been feeling apprehensive about this conversation.

Kai rakes his fingers through his long blond hair and blinks fast, like he's trying to process this new information. In an instant, fury rages through his nostrils and, without warning, he swings his fist at Logan hoping to knock him out. Luckily, I manage to block him but he doesn't stop. We end up wrestling next to Logan, who doesn't do anything but stands next to us, looking guilty.

"Let me crush him! Orion, let me go! I want to break his face. If Maisy had stayed with me she would have been safe! None of this would have happened!"

"Kai, calm down!" I hiss as I grapple with him.

"Don't you get it? Nobody knew where she was. I was gonna take her away from here...For fuck's sake, O-Ryon! Let-me-go!" The anger sparks out of him.

"Kai, if you hadn't taken her, something else would have happened for sure. Maybe Maisy would have been killed, who knows? But it's done now. It's over!" I growl. When you put things in perspective, people tend to see better. And there it is, Kai slows down, and backs off.

"If it makes you feel better, hit me. I can take it." Logan wants to atone for his grave mistake.

"No! For fuck's sake! Nobody's gonna be hitting anybody!" I let go of Kai and fix my messy hair, although as a precaution I'm still standing between them. "Kai, all of us were dealing with stuff we didn't know how to deal with. And for that, we paid the price. Logan and I nearly died, Maisy got taken and you, you were hiding for months behind your guilt."

Kai's nostrils are still flared, and his brows knitted together. "So the Slavs didn't kill twenty men in your house that night? It was a Vitali?"

"Lukash, the Vitali hitman, got paid a million dollars to deliver Maisy alive to the Slav HQ. It was the Slavs that did that." I retort.

Kai's eyes glint with revenge as he regards me, and then Logan.

"Fucking greedy bastard!" he says through gritted teeth.

"I wouldn't worry about him, he got what he deserved." Logan mutters darkly.

"His wife, too." I add.

Seeing that Kai's hormones have settled down, Logan pulls a bottle of whiskey from the drinks cabinet. We've emptied quite a few since I've been staying here. Poor Uncle Jon; he's tasked with replenishing our stock and because of it, he's been busting our asses. We shouldn't drink while recuperating from surgery, but fuck that. While we're up here in the penthouse and planning the dominion of New York, I'll drink as much as I want. We ain't got a drink problem. We got a Slav problem.

Kai settles onto the couch and I take a seat next to him. Logan passes around the glasses and fills them to the brim with a steady pour. He leaves the bottle on the coffee table and sits on the other side of Kai.

"To... us."

I raise my glass and down it in one. They do the same.

"More?" Logan asks.

"More," Kai says, and I nod in agreement.

Logan goes through the same motions until we've drunk the second glass in full. That's when the awkward silence ensues.

How the fuck do we tell him about the letter from Marina? How do you start that kind of conversation?

"Third time lucky?" Logan offers. He's stalling. Kai snickers and I just hand over my glass complicitly.

But just as I see Logan about to offer a fourth round, I raise my hand. "That's enough."

Kai holds up his empty glass. "One more." It's clear to me that he's been drinking more than usual lately.

"Orion's right," Logan says.

Kai looks at me, suddenly noticing what I'm wearing, then at Logan. "What's this, the sweatpants gang?"

"When you've been shot, it's comfort over style, Kai," I tell him. "At least while you're recovering." True, I'm not happy about it, but I know very soon I'll be back in my three-piece suit. Right now, I look just like a domestic gun for hire.

"I'm sure I can find a pair of sweatpants for you somewhere. You'll need them for Long Island," Logan needles Kai. "I heard you spent the whole time in your boxer shorts."

"Seriously, I'm not used to seeing you like this. We have a war coming and we gotta be ready," Kai says.

His somber words bring me back to the circumstances we're in. "Damn right we have a war coming. But before getting into it, there's something we gotta tell you." I glance at Logan.

Kai's brow furrows and he closes his eyes. "I don't think I'm ready to hear about Maisy yet. If you don't want me to run to the Slavs this very minute, kill everyone there, and probably die, don't tell me. I just... I can't."

"It's not about Maisy. It's about... us."

"What about us?"

"I should've said something sooner. But I wanted to see you and tell you in person, I..."

"Goddammit, Orion! Spit it out!"

I look at Logan, who's nodding sympathetically.

"Just before all hell broke loose with Maisy, do you remember that night I got a package from Marina?"

Kai's eyes narrow; he looks at me, then at Logan. "Go on."

"Well, last time I spoke to her, I asked her to compare our DNA."

He gapes at me. "Fuck! I had the letter in my hand the night I found you, but I stupidly threw it away."

"Well, that letter had the results."

"Are you gonna tell me we're related?" Kai asks, but doesn't let me respond. "Look, Orion, I trusted Marina a lot, but really? If that letter says we're brothers, who's to say someone else didn't do this, and is setting us up for something we got no idea about? The question we should be asking ourselves is, what do they have to gain by giving us this piece of information?"

"That's what I've been saying all along, Kai," Logan tells him. "But we did another test, and got the same results."

Kai stands up without a word and begins to stride around the room, seemingly lost in thought. I know he's trying to figure this all out, but even I have no idea how it happened.

Finally, he looks at us and sits his ass back down on the couch. "So it's true? We're half-brothers?" he asks, his voice tinged with a hint of fear.

I nod. "I'm afraid so."

"Fuck."

Logan snorts. "That's the gist of it."

Kai shakes his head, a sly smirk on his lips. "That means we went down a notch."

"What do you mean?"

"You two became my *brothers* that day we met, years ago," Kai says. "And now that you turned out to be my *half*-brothers, you went down a notch. Meaning, I don't have to give my life for you anymore, fuckers!" he finishes with a grin.

Logan laughs while I observe Kai. He's taking this news light-heartedly. I chuckle. "That's true. We're already connected. A piece of paper won't change that."

"But if you'd died two months ago, I'd never have found out about it," Kai adds.

Logan pats him on the shoulder. "You saved us. And we're grateful."

"Right now, I'm still fighting the demons inside me who insist I should hit you, man. Why *the fuck* you called a hit on Maisy, you asshole!"

"I was in a bad place that night, Kai. I'm sorry, man. What else can I say?"

Kai tries to sympathize with Logan but it's hard for him, I see it on his face. "What about our mother?"

Logan shrugs. "Imagine that. I've been searching for her all my life, and here she was, giving me half-brothers left right and center."

I scowl at him. "Watch your mouth, Logan. That's my mother you're talking about."

"What, you gonna fight me, too?" he teases.

"If I have to. I don't let anyone talk shit about my family."

Kai pours himself another glass of whiskey. He fills it to the brim, picks it up, and leans back in his seat. "Okay, but how? How is this possible?"

"Rebecca Trellis. That's our mother," Logan says. "The woman who gave us our middle names. And we all know what those mean. Why?"

"Maisy said there was something about her in a newspaper, she saw it in Milan's office," I interject. "That's all we know."

"What's it about?" Kai asks.

"Fuck knows," I say.

"Did our fathers know each other?"

"Naah. They knew of each other, but they hated each other's guts with a vengeance," Logan replies.

"So how did our mother manage to fool three of the smartest, cruelest, and most savage men in New

York?" Kai wonders. "Do you think she had help from Milan?"

We look at each other. *Fuck.*

"Do you think she was a Slav?" Kai's question annoys me.

"What the fuck, Kai?" I snap. I don't even want to entertain the thought. And yet, it's in my head now.

"That's our mother you're talking about!" Logan reprimands him.

"Hey, imagine if Maisy's our–"

"Stop it!" I growl. "That's enough!"

All of a sudden, we're interrupted by multiple buzzes of the interphone. The button is being pressed furiously. Our eyes meet and then we're up on our feet, alert.

Uncle Jon appears from the other room. "Have you checked the interphone?"

"Doing it right now." Logan runs to the intercom station and Kai and I join him. Whoever's buzzing, they're in a hurry.

"Don't you have someone at reception?" Kai asks, looking confused. I am too, as I know Logan's men are there.

"Fuck. This is worrying," Logan says, waiting impatiently for the video to turn on.

The moment it's up on the little screen, we all stare at it as if spellbound, even Uncle Jon. Someone who looks exactly like Maisy is pressing the button in a panic, and judging by the contortion of her face, she's crying. No, screaming. We hear no sound, yet I can tell bullets are being fired past her, ending up embedded in the wall behind her.

Logan pushes the intercom button and the sound of the mayhem downstairs is broadcast directly into the penthouse, including Maisy's terrified voice.

"Open the elevator! Please, open it!" she pleads over the gunfire as more bullets fly past her head.

Logan activates the elevator doors and she runs inside. Lucky for her, the doors shut just before two goons reach her, though they try in vain to open them by force.

We're watching the screen like it's a movie, the intensity making me momentarily forget to breathe. "What the fuck is happening downstairs?" I ask quietly.

The men focus all their strength on opening the elevator, but not a minute passes before they're mowed down by a machine gun. I see some of the bullets ricochetting off the metal doors.

Logan switches the camera angle, and I see that it's one of my men with the machine gun. When the view swaps back to the elevator, the dead bogeys are now being dragged away by their feet.

"Is everything okay down there?" Uncle Jon is talking to someone on his cell. "Right. Okay. Thank you."

"Well?" Logan asks.

"It's the girl. She ran inside the tower with the Slavs shooting at her. She's lucky we're prepping for a war or she'd have died trying to get up here."

"Was that really her?" Kai asks, like he doesn't trust what he saw.

"It looked like her," I say.

Logan paces up and down in front of the elevator, nervously waiting for it to reach the top floor, to reach us.

Finally, the door pings and slowly begins to open. Too slow, if you ask me. The three of us draw our guns, aim at the elevator, and wait.

"How the fuck did she manage to escape the Slavs?" Uncle Jon mutters.

"Uncle Jon!" Logan snarls.

Jon holds his hands up and takes a few steps backward. "I'm just saying." He turns and goes back to his office.

I'm ready to rain hell on whoever's inside, but I find myself blindly pointing my gun at... Maisy. Or a girl who looks exactly like her. Her hair's just about touching her shoulders, shorter than before; her clothes are torn, she has cuts and bruises all over her, and she's smeared with blood, dried blood, mostly on her arms. In stunned silence, I glance at Kai, then Logan, then back at her.

She stares at us with wide, dark eyes, her chest heaving, just like that day we first met her, until her eyes roll back in her head and she faints, falling at our feet.

"Maisy!" I crouch to check her pulse. "Fuck!"

"Maisy, stay with us." Logan checks under her eyelids, but I don't know what he's checking for.

I lift her into my arms and carry her to the living room. I lay her gently on the couch and we stand over her for a few moments, the three of us sharing a quiet pause.

"Is this a déjà vu moment or am I losing my mind?" Kai murmurs.

She's been through hell; it looks like a lot of the blood is from her arm.

"How the fuck did she get away?" Logan asks.

"Let's figure that out when she wakes up," I say as I take a good look at Maisy. Her sleeveless black dress is torn up, and the bruises really are all over her body. She reeks, too, if I'm honest. Dammit, I hate that she looks hurt, and innocent, lying here unconscious. I bet she's not. She can't be. I know I said she belongs to us, and she does, but a Slav is still a Slav. And she better have a really good explanation for how she got away from there. We tried several times to get her back, and failed. Most likely because we had to assign the job to men who were not willing to die for her. Assholes.

"Call your men, Kai. Logan, get Uncle Jon to tell everyone to be on high alert. I'll call the Cartes to come here and stay on guard until we know what we're doing. And we better think of something fast. They won't stop until they get Maisy."

I sit on the chair opposite her and take out my cell to text Uncle Colletti and Uncle Leo. Everyone will be deployed. That was the last time I let those Slavs fuck us around. "Logan, you need to examine her."

"Let me tell Uncle Jon to inform everyone, and then I'll get my medical kit."

LOGAN

Either this woman is the most cunning woman in the world and playing us like fiddles, or this is just her fucking luck.

I sit next to her and stroke her face. She's lost weight. She's bruised, with way too many cuts on her skin, and she's dirty. Her hair is greasy. She smells awful, too. Her dress is torn and her shoulders are reddened from her blood. I slowly move her arm, checking where the dried blood might have come from.

As I move to examine her, I notice her chest starts rising rapidly. She's having a panic attack.

"Hey, hey. Maisy, shhh..." I whisper. "Take a deep breath. You're with us, sweetheart. I don't know how, but you're here, with us."

She calms down when she hears my voice, and her eyelids flutter open. She smiles at me. "Am I... Am I dead?" she breathes.

I grin at her. "They can't kill us that easy, sweetheart."

Kai hasn't moved from her side. He towers above her, drinking in her presence.

Her gaze lands on him. "Kai," she whispers.

"Hey, baby girl." He tries to sound comforting.

Her eyes gloss over. "O-Orion?"

I ignore her question. I have to make sure she's okay. "Do you mind if I check you over?"

"I-I'm fine." She slowly sits up, groaning in pain as she does, and her eyes find Orion. "Orion!" She smiles through her tears and wipes them from her cheeks. "You're alive!"

"Missed me, darling?" Orion smirks.

Her smile quickly turns into a frown. Her chin wobbles and more tears spill from beneath her eyelashes. "I-I thought you died. I saw you getting shot." She covers her face with her hands and weeps.

"Hey, we're here." I put my arm around her shoulders, allowing her head to nestle in the crook of my neck.

Kai sits next to her. "Maisy, how did you know we'd be here?"

"I-I didn't. I just saw the tower and knew it was Vitali Tower, from... from the last time, when I ended up downstairs, in your studio. I knew I could find help here."

"Let me quickly check your arm," I cut in, and take a closer look. It appears that the dry blood is from her implant having been cut out.

She pulls her arm from my grip. "Ouch!"

"When did this happen?" I ask.

"Six or seven weeks ago. At the doctor's. They just cut it out. It still hurts like hell."

"Seven weeks ago?! It must be infected. There may be something still inside. Let me see." I notice a small protrusion. "The implant must've broken as they were taking it out." I check my bag for tweezers.

"Um... have they hurt you?" Kai asks, like he's bracing himself for whatever she'll say.

I am too. Anyone who laid a finger on her will end up dead. That's my promise.

"Nuh-uh. They were waiting for me to get my period before they could all, um, breed... rape me." Her voice wobbles as she finishes.

"But they haven't, right? You haven't got your period yet?" he asks hesitantly.

"No. They were taking me to the doctor because of it. That's when I got away."

"Stupid men. There's no need to wait for your period. The moment the implant's out, you can get pregnant. But thank fuck they had no idea. Let me deal with your arm now." I approach her wound with my tweezers. "Mm-hmm, it's definitely your implant. Don't move." I know I need to be quick because it will hurt like hell. The infection is looking nasty.

I pinch the tiny remainder of the implant with my tweezers and extract it quickly, just before she screams and pushes me away.

"Logan, what the fuck are you doing to her?!" Orion shoots to his feet, ready to fight for her as she jumps into Kai's lap, crying.

"I had to take it out. It's infected."

"Then be gentle!" he growls. "Maisy? You okay?"

She nods. "It hurts. Like there's fire under my skin."

"I gotta sterilize it now," I warn. "That'll hurt like hell too."

She starts sobbing again, but this time offers her arm to me.

"I'll be as fast as I can, I promise." I pour pure alcohol over the wound, making sure it gets everywhere it needs to as her sobs rapidly become loud wails.

"That's it. I'm done. It's over now," I say as I put a large bandage on it.

She burrows into Kai's arms as he wipes her tears. "It's okay, Maisy," he whispers.

The four of us stay silent for a while, unsure of where and how to proceed from here. Maisy's somehow with us again, and we didn't even have to take a bullet to make it happen. She just came to us. Luck? I hope it is.

Orion's the one to break the silence. "Maisy, tell us what happened to you?"

She sniffles. "The man who shot you took me to Rosey's. After she paid him, she threw me in a filthy cell in the basement."

"Don't worry, he got what he deserved. Greedy fucking asshole!" I murmur.

"They were taking me to the doctor's today. When I saw Vitali Tower, I jumped out of the car." She shrugs. "I took my chance."

Kai tightens his embrace and slowly strokes her hair as she cuddles into his chest. Fuck, what I wouldn't give to be in his place. Maisy is the oxygen coursing through my veins.

I pick up the bottle from the table and fill our glasses with whiskey.

"Can I have a glass?" Maisy asks quietly.

Orion and I share a glance.

"You drink whiskey?" Kai asks.

"I don't want it. I need it. Something to cleanse the bitter taste from my mouth. And calm my soul. I've been alone all this time."

I pull out a fresh glass and fill it for Maisy. She picks it up, salutes us as we raise our glasses, and all of us down our shots.

"Um, Logan, when I last saw you…" She turns to me, looking bolder than before. "Was that true, what the man said? Were you gonna hand me over after our last time together?"

"No!" I say.

"Fuck no, Maisy," Orion growls.

"Then… were you not gonna come get me?" she asks, looking between all three of us.

"We would have. You know we would." Kai rushes to respond like a teenager in love. Not that all of us aren't, but she needs assurance, not desperation. Plus, he doesn't know that we did try to get her back.

"Maisy, sweetheart, we tried. Orion and I planned, sent our men, but they couldn't penetrate the Slavs HQ. And with us still recuperating, it was an impossible feat." I say. "We only just got Kai back today, for the first time in two months."

"You did?" Her brows crook. "Where were you, Kai?"

"I was… I was out of commission. Feeling sorry for myself, fucked up. Our plan was to annihilate the

Slavs, and instead, they got you." Kai nods in my direction. "And all the other shit that happened. I just couldn't handle it, baby girl."

"Eventually we'd have gotten you back, Maisy. We just didn't know you'd beat us to it." Orion reassures her.

She leans into Kai's chest again. "I haven't had a shower all this time. They didn't let me wash up. They told me some men preferred me dirty. They were just waiting for the right time."

None of us seem to know what to say.

"I'm sorry for reeking of garbage."

"Don't worry, baby girl. You don't smell at all," Kai comforts her.

"What's important is that they didn't harm you. As for the smell, that's easy. Shall I run you a bath?" I offer. I search for her eyes, and upon landing in her abyss, smile at her.

She nods and starts to get off Kai's lap. "I'd love to. I just wanna be clean."

"Can you manage by yourself?" Kai asks.

"I think so."

I spring to my feet, quickly grasping her hand. "Are you hungry?"

"No. Maybe I'll have something later if you don't mind."

"Sure. Anytime."

I take Maisy to Orion's room to use his ensuite. It has the biggest bath as well as a shower. "Take off your dress, and feel free to throw it out. I'll get someone to get your clothes from Orion's house. Is that okay?"

"Sure." She strips down to nothing in a blink. I notice how bony her body is; it's different from months ago. Also, very dirty.

I lean down to prepare her bath, but seeing her naked body rouses the usual fire inside me. My sweatpants twitch from my cock growing so fast.

Once I'm happy with the temperature of the water, I straighten up.

"Have a nice bath, Maisy." I stroke her cheek and she leans into my hand. "I'm glad you're here. With us. It's saved us the trouble of getting shot at again."

She smiles. "You're funny."

"I'm gonna leave now, or else I'd have to take a bath with you. Your towels are here." I point to the one hanging on the rail, getting warm. "And everything else you need, you'll find in the cabinet. I'll see you when you're finished."

I leave her to it and close the door behind me. Back in the living room, I find both Kai and Orion sitting in tense silence.

"What did I miss?"

"This idiot here got me doubting everything," Orion grumbles.

"I only said 'imagine if Maisy is…' I could've meant a ton of stuff."

"We have a spare kit, right?" I remind Orion.

"Of course." Orion heads for the shelves next to the TV and picks up a few boxes. He opens one and passes it to Kai. "Here, swab a sample from inside your cheek and get it ready for send-off. Let's double check your DNA."

"You got one for Maisy?" Kai asks.

"Here it is. Logan, go get a swab from her right now. I want the results tonight."

"Sure. Before I forget, can you get someone to bring her clothes from your house? Like, as soon as possible?"

"The Cartes are staying in my house. I can arrange for them to be delivered in the next half hour." Orion pulls out his cell and starts texting.

"Kai, I want you to take the DNA samples to a lab. I'll text you the address. And wait there until they're done. Is that okay?"

"Sure."

CHAPTER 8

MAISY

The sight of Orion's and Logan's bodies, crumpled and lifeless in a pool of blood, is something I never want to be faced with again. At that very moment, my whole world collapsed.

The echo of gunshots reverberated in my ears and tears blurred my vision as the man dragged me away.

Even if I wanted to run, there wasn't any place for me to go to. Rosey wanted me. The Slavs wanted me. The only way out was to die.

But I didn't. The darkness of that basement was my home. I barely slept or ate. I was terrified that at any moment, the Slavs would storm in and rape me. Make more Slav babies. I had panic attacks, and my chest hurt with every ragged breath I took down there. Because it also reminded me of my time there with Logan. The time when Marina got killed right in front of my eyes.

I felt utterly alone and abandoned.

I wished Orion and Logan were alive, but as the days stretched into eternity, despair crept in and I gave up hope. Then I began to wonder, if Kai was alive, where was he?

Being all alone for what seemed like forever, I realized there was something new developing inside me, some kind of spark of defiance, something that refused to be defeated.

Rage maybe, similar to Orion's. I was angry at what my life had turned out to be.

And it started the moment I was taken to the Slavs, to the house Rosey had taken over. The men who met me at the entrance were vile; they kept groping me and all of them told me how they couldn't wait to put a baby in me. It was Rosey who saved me from their grubby hands. I kept thinking *she's good, she'll be there for me, she's my sister,* but I forgot what I am to them. Actually, to her. A vessel for bearing children. Milan brainwashed her thoroughly. My sister. I will never forgive myself for that.

I was taken to the basement where I spent the following two months. Lucky for me, my cell was locked, because every Slav had access to the basement, and they used it too. They'd come at all times of day to jerk off, telling me they couldn't wait to get their hands on me. To defile me.

On my first day there, a man in a white coat came and, rather roughly, cut my arm and removed my implant. Then, he'd check me daily for my period. He'd touch me between my legs, and sometimes his fingers would slip inside me. He probably expected a different reaction than retching, but it was nauseating enough having him in my cell.

I asked Rosey what her plans for me were, and she responded with a frightening honesty. She wanted to get me pregnant as soon as possible; she'd had enough of having babies. *It's your turn now*, she said.

With my period still missing after two months, the Slavs became impatient. That's when they decided to take me to a real doctor, I think.

But I never got there. Was it luck? I don't know. All I know is that the moment I saw Vitali Tower through the window, I knew I had to jump. I opened the door and threw myself out. Then, I ran. I ran like hell.

Logan just took a swab of my DNA; I didn't ask why. Whatever it is, I'll do it. Are they trying to see if I'm really a Slav? And could there be a chance that I'm not?

He muttered something about going downstairs to see what the damage is in the reception area, in the aftermath of me getting inside.

Wherever I go, death and destruction follow me, but hopefully not anymore. Now that I'm here, I'm never leaving this place. The bath has been the best thing so far. I've scrubbed my body clean from … from the Slavs. Although I know I cannot swap my blood with someone else's. I am who I am. At least now I'm clean. I shaved too. I had so much hair on me, it was ungodly. And finally, I got to brush my teeth. Now I smell fresh, like peonies or lavender - who knows? All I know is that I'm clean.

Before I exit the bathroom, I take the plug out. The color of the water is vile and I scrub the bath clean. I want no evidence here of my time in that basement.

Once I'm finished, I wrap my body in the white Egyptian cotton towel Logan left for me. I sigh from the luxurious feeling that encases my body. Then, I towel-dry and brush my hair. It's shorter now, just about touching my shoulders, unevenly cut. Rosey did it herself. She must see me as her competition because she hoped it would make me look uglier. I don't care how I look.

I step back into the living area, and this time I get a better look at the grandeur that surrounds me. Orion is by himself, sitting on the couch and looking at his cell.

"Where's Kai?" I ask.

He raises his head, fixing his gaze on me. He watches me with a mixture of adoration and longing. Being watched like that makes me feel like I'm free to show my vulnerability and desire at the same time. Orion does something to me on a different level.

"He's running an errand for me," he replies, setting his cell on the coffee table. He leans back and takes his time regarding me.

I'm drawn by the mesmerizing view that stretches before me and I approach the floor-to-ceiling windows, admiring the city lights. We're so high up, it's like being cut off from the real world.

I'm not sure how long I've been standing like this, loving everything before me like the true New York girl I am, when in the reflection of the glass, I see Orion behind me. He gently wraps his arm around my waist, pulling me flush to his body. With his other hand, he moves my hair out of the way and kisses down my neck. "Maisy, darling, how I missed you," he whispers in my ear, before inhaling deeply.

I lean back into his shoulder. I need someone holding me, telling me I was missed, that my nightmare will be over soon.

The city below fades into insignificance as I turn to face him, my soul and body laid bare in front of him. Right now, he is the beacon of hope in the darkness that threatens to engulf me.

I press my lips to his. "I missed you too."

He responds with a soft hum before devouring my mouth, weaving his tongue around mine, swallowing my moans fully before he moves his lips down my neck and buries his face in it.

He unties my towel and allows it to drop to the floor. Then he lowers himself to my breasts, holds them in the palms of his hands, and tugs my nipples between his teeth, one then the other, stoking the fire burning inside me. He's hungry for me; I hear it in his groans as he devours my body with his tongue. Then, unexpectedly, he kneels before me and lifts one of my legs, resting my thigh on his shoulder to give him better access. He grins up at me wickedly before giving me a full, wet lick from my perineum up to my clit.

My leg buckles and I lean back against the cold glass for support. The way I'm burning up, I think it may melt under my touch.

All my nerve endings awaken. He does it again, but this time he ends up sucking me, bringing me near to culmination in seconds. He does it *again*, making spiraling movements with his tongue as I wait in suspense, and always ending on my clit, torturing me into oblivion.

My hands weave into his hair and I grip his head, pressing him against me as he eats me like a French gateau. I'm flying and moaning. My hips twist and move against his tongue and I'm chasing my release when, suddenly, I sense his tongue going up. When he lowers my leg to the floor, I know he's not going back there.

I moan in protest, try to push him down, but he's not having it. Instead, he blazes a wet trail up my body, between my breasts and up my neck, reaching my gaping mouth and forcefully pressing his tongue inside it as his fingers curl under my knee and lift my leg again. He pulls down his sweatpants and his thick, rigid, pierced cock slides urgently into me, to the hilt.

"Fuck - me! You - little - slut... How - much - I - craved - your - wet - cunt!"

With each word comes a hard, brutal thrust, bringing me closer to heaven. Is it possible that ten, maybe fifteen thrusts are enough for me to orgasm? My juices run down my thighs as he pushes into me, my back flat against the window. He uses it for leverage as he lifts my other leg, and keeps pounding me with hungry, low grunts while I feel every vein in his stealthy cock that I have been missing so much for all this time. I'm stretched, wet, and close to the edge and Orion doesn't show any sign of slowing down. I'm still held in his arms, pinned to the glass, and his thrusts come in hard as he pounds me with all his strength.

This is bliss; he's coming at me harder with every stroke and I'm losing myself. The pleasure is exhilarating, and I feel my peak begin to arrive in waves. I pull him close with my legs, wrapping them around his body, and let him thrust even deeper into me. I feel him stilling inside me and he grunts my name while my body tightens around him, and I'm convulsing, reaching my explosion too, burying my face in his neck to stifle my moans.

We stay in this position until our breathing evens out, connected and sated, until I sense I'm about to slip down the glass.

"Orion, don't let me fall!" I shriek, laughing.

"Fall? Never." He strengthens his hold on me by placing his hand under my butt cheek, then pulls out of me to fix his cock in his sweatpants with his other hand, before finally placing it under my other cheek while I wrap my legs and arms tightly around his body.

He turns us around and takes me to the couch, gently setting me down on the cushions. Only now do I see Logan sitting in the adjacent chair, fire smoldering in his eyes.

Orion goes back to where we were fucking, picks up my towel, and then returns to cover me with it. "Until your clothes arrive, which should be any minute now."

All sweaty, he sits down on the couch next to me and takes off his t-shirt, revealing his six-pack, tattooed torso, and the patch of bandaging across his body. I feel my cheeks heat up. For some reason, all this is a little awkward.

"Sweetheart, are you blushing?" Logan teases. I don't want to look in his eyes, because now I know my face is red. "Oh, come on, you've done nastier stuff than fucking by a window."

I cover my grin with my hands. *Why am I getting flustered?* "Or was that not nasty *enough*?" he continues. "I'm sure the doctor can arrange something."

The buzzing of the intercom saves me.

Logan chuckles and stands up. "To be continued."

Orion regards me too, and as our eyes meet, he takes my chin in his hand and pulls me to him. He presses his lips to mine and gives me a soft, unhurried kiss. I love these kisses. They're full of emotion, and they promise a lot.

I hear Logan in the background. "Yes?"

"Boss, Maisy's clothes are here," comes a voice I don't know. "I'll put them in the elevator."

"Sure, send them up," Logan responds.

"Thank you!" I whisper, ending the kiss with Orion. I stand up, fix the towel around my body, and go to the elevator to wait for my stuff.

"Feeling better?" Logan asks.

I nod. "Mm-hmm."

"Ready for more?"

I smile at him. *Of course I'm ready.*

"Sweetheart, I can't wait to fuck you. My cock literally hurts for you."

I'm grinning again. *They still want me.*

"Patience, doctor," I say, just as the elevator pings. I run inside, open the bag, and rummage through it, searching for black panties and a black cami. I find them and, still in the elevator, drop my towel and quickly get dressed. Then I grab the bag and towel and leave the elevator.

I look at Logan. "Where am I sleeping?"

He crooks an eyebrow. "What makes you think you'll be sleeping at all?"

"Okay." I laugh. "Where do I take these?"

"Straight down the corridor, Maisy," Orion says. "My room."

I stick my tongue out at Logan and walk toward Orion's room to the sound of Logan snickering.

"Missed your round ass!" he calls after me.

CHAPTER 9

ORION

"Maisy, once you drop off your clothes, come back here. We gotta talk about something," I tell Maisy as she walks past me.

"Sure."

This is it. No more lying and fuck knows what. Logan sits up in his chair; he, too, knows it's time we ask her.

The elevator pings again and both of us crane our necks to look. Kai's back. *Perfect timing.*

"Where's Maisy?" He doesn't say anything about the results. That's not important in his world, but where he'll stick his cock tonight is.

"She'll be back in a minute. You got the results?" I ask.

"I do." He sits on the other chair, looking all serious. "There's not an easy way to say this."

I fix him with an intense stare, sending a clear message that I'm not in the mood for any humor or games right now.

Logan's worried. "Kai?"

"I'm not sure how to break this to you."

"Stop fucking about, Kai," I growl.

He looks at me, then at Logan, then shakes his head. "At least now you'll have a good reason to kick my ass, as it turns out I really am your half-brother." He grins.

Logan guffaws. "Idiot!"

"That's long overdue!" I agree. "And Maisy's results?"

He sighs and removes his leather jacket before saying anything else. From the pocket, he takes a piece of paper and unfolds it.

"What does it say?" Logan glances at me, uncertain. "Kai, I swear, I'm gonna fuck you up if you're playing around."

"Why would I play around with this?"

Kai is annoying the hell out of me right now, and any further conversation with him will just rile me more.

"I shouldn't have joked about her," he says as he passes me the paper.

My eyes bore into him. He better not try to joke.

"What does that mean?!" Logan needs answers, and I do too.

I take the piece of paper and start reading. And I see it right there. The results. I close my eyes, crazily relieved, and start to think of many different ways to discipline Kai.

He thinks he's funny, playing with us. Well, with my patience wearing thin, he's in for a surprise.

I exchange a glance with Logan as Kai's laughter rings out like a taunt, pushing me to the brink of my restraint.

With a swift movement, I lunge forward, my fingers curling around Kai's wrists like steel. Logan follows suit, and even with Kai as big and strong as he is, our combined strength overpowers our reckless younger brother. *Correction: half-brother.*

Kai's laughter falters as we pull him onto the couch and hold him captive, his bravado crumbling by the second. I'm furious, so is Logan, and we both know what true torment is yet to come to Kai.

"Force his mouth open!" I order, and Logan pushes his fingers inside his cheeks. Kai's mouth is pulled open. I grin and make out like I'm going to spit into his gaping mouth. My saliva drools while Kai shakes off Logan's grip and bucks underneath us.

"No! Orion, don't do it! I'm sorry! I really am! Fuck!" Kai's apology means nothing; I want him to experience the panic I went through when I was reading the letter, although I know we're not kids anymore, and he's gonna hate me forever if I actually spit in his mouth. We used to roughhouse like this when we were young, but we should know better now.

"What shall we do to him, Logan?"

"I know!" Logan exclaims. "No sex with Maisy. For a *week*."

"No! No way!" Kai protests, and opens his mouth. "Spit. Go on, I don't care. Spit in my mouth. Assholes. Do it!"

I frown at him. "*We're* the assholes?"

"Wh-What are you doing?" Maisy's angelic voice suddenly cuts through the testosterone frenzy on the couch.

"Just fooling around." Logan goes back to where he was sitting, but I've still got Kai pinned underneath me.

"That was not funny." I smack his head before I get off him and go to sit in the chair where he was.

"The looks on your faces, though." Kai fixes his hair and smirks. "Priceless."

"What happened?" Maisy asks him.

"Just clowning around. Never mind. Come and sit next to me before these two change their minds and kick the shit out of me."

Maisy plops her bottom on the couch and giggles. "They wouldn't."

"What makes you think we won't punish him for what he did?" I ask.

"What did he do?"

"You don't remember? He kidnapped you when he shouldn't have," Logan says.

"Oh."

"Well? Why do you think we shouldn't punish him?"

She shrugs. "Because you're good friends... and... I dunno."

I nod. "I think you *do* know."

"I... know?"

"Sweetheart, we know you know," Logan says encouragingly. Like me, he wants her to just come out and say *because you're half-brothers.*

"I know... what?"

"*Does* she know?" Kai inspects her expression closely for any signs of recognition and seems to come to a conclusion. "Yeah, she must do."

"I don't know what you're talking about. Honestly." Her sweet, innocent voice is like honey. *Luring me in.*

The three of us stare at her quietly for a tad too long.

"Maisy, did you know we're half-brothers?" I finally ask.

I watch her carefully, because I want to detect every minute movement on her face. Deception requires significant skill, of which she has an abundance.

Her eyes go wide, and all she mutters is, "Oh. That."

"*That?!*" After being totally sated by her sweet cunt only a half hour ago, right now I could strangle her for her nonchalant reaction. "*THAT?!*"

"Orion," Logan warns.

I know I'm about to lose control. *But really, "that"?*

"Um, I..." She looks at us, one by one, before her eyes drop to look at her hands. "I-I met your mother. Briefly." She's fumbling with her fingers, and her voice is barely audible. "I wasn't sure she was telling me the truth. At the time, all I knew about you was that you'd kill anyone who'd dare to mention you might belong to a different mafia family."

She lifts her eyes and, seeing us so still, watching her so intently, she quickly lowers them again.

"We were together in that basement for a couple of hours. Me and your mother. I found out she was kept down there for years."

Logan shifts in his chair, agitated. His left eye twitches. I'm disturbed, too. Maisy is finally coming clean and some of it, I know, will not be easy to hear. *She was kept there for years?*

"She made me promise." She raises her gaze to the three of us again, looking at us one by one, and reiterates. "She made me *promise* to tell you that even though her life was all about vengeance, that she meant harm with every breath she took, after everything your families did to her family, she really, really loved you."

"Why didn't you tell us?" Kai asks her.

"If I had told you that the moment I met you, you'd have killed me on the spot for coming to you with such a crazy theory. And I wasn't sure if she was telling the truth until recently, when I found out about being a Slav. I saw the newspaper article in Milan's old office. Which I left for you on the bed, when Kai and I took off that night. You didn't see it?"

"No. Please, continue," I say, my chest tightening as I wait anxiously for what comes next.

"Four generations of bystanders killed in a shootout on Good Friday! Rebecca Trellis, 12, the only survivor of a family of over 40 members, is in a critical condition."

"On Easter, thirty-three years ago, they all died except her. She was sent to a foster care, and from there, for a long time planned her vengeance. She was clever. She slept with your fathers, one by one, gave birth to you all, and offered them custody, under one condition: that she could give you your middle names. Her plan was to have a child with Milan too, and then stand aside and watch you all kill each other. But by the time she got pregnant by Milan, she found out that he wasn't a Slavinovich. So she aborted it. That's when her plan fell apart. Milan never got over losing his unborn baby, and he became obsessive and suspicious of her."

"And then, she told me, depression got to her. She couldn't get her babies out of her mind. All of you. Milan caught her exchanging emails and messages with Mickey Delgado. And that was it. He took her to the basement and after torturing her for weeks, she told him everything. Milan loved your mother's plan, he thought it was genius. And he made sure none of you found out about it."

Maisy pauses for a moment.

"Kai, she was one of your nannies."

"I don't remember her," Kai interrupts, looking uncomfortable. As if he's embarrassed about the times he spoke about his nannies like a spoiled brat.

She turns to him. "She told your father she wanted you back. That she'd take Logan and Orion too and leave New York with the three of you. Take you away from this life. That's why Milan killed him. Your father knew this, Kai. When he was dying in the hospital, he wanted to tell someone about it. Marina's husband happened to be the last person who talked to him.

Mickey Delgado mentioned the date of the Good Friday shootout as he was dying, and that got Marina's husband killed. Milan didn't want anyone finding out about your mother's genius plan.

"What happened to her?" I ask.

"She died in the basement. When I saw her, she was taking her last breaths. That's when she told me everything, when she made me promise to unite you. I saw her the day she died."

"So our mother died... when we met you?" Logan asks.

"Yes. That day, I was taken by Camila to the Slav HQ, Milan's house. While she was looking for Zed, she left me on my own. And I wanted to run to a place where no one would find me. I heard Rebecca's cries, so instead of jumping the wall, I went to the basement to see what was going on. Zed caught me talking to her, and as he dragged me away, he kicked her. That was the final straw for her. She died, and I was taken away to be prepped as one of his whores. That's when I ran away and went to your house for help. Or to kill Camila. I dunno."

"Why didn't you come clean when you saw us?" Kai obviously wants to know why all the lies. I do too.

"I needed protection. I wanted to tell you, but you caught me lying so many times. And Rebecca made me promise that when you did find out, you wouldn't kill each other. *'Help them untangle from the pain and hatred I spun around them'* were her words."

Maisy's gaze drops back to her hands when she stops talking. It seems that she's finished telling her story.

I take the whiskey bottle and refill the four glasses that are still on the table.

I pick up my glass and down it in one. Logan and Kai follow, both finishing their drinks swiftly. Maisy goes last; she takes her glass, sips a little, and then gently sets it back on the table.

"Wow," Logan mutters. He looks shocked. I think we all are.

Our mother... She planned her vengeance from the age of twelve. If that doesn't scream mafia, I don't know what does.

I stand up and rake my fingers through my hair. I don't know how I feel about any of this. I stride over to the windows overlooking Manhattan and stare down at the view. Trying to make sense of it all.

"How did you find out?" Maisy asks quietly.

"We got Marina to compare our DNA," Kai replies. "You'd given us enough clues."

I'm overwhelmed. My head will probably explode from the information overload. Plus my cock's still twitching from Maisy's proximity. I've missed her badly all this time, and I bet Logan and Kai feel the same.

I look back at them and notice Logan's eyes are closed. Okay, maybe he's thinking about our mother, Rebecca Trellis. What fucking luck she had. To lose everyone at the age of twelve, *everyone*, and end up in foster care. And then do what? Create three lives and hope they'll kill each other one day? I have mixed feelings about her already. She played the long game. Her approach to revenge involved patience and long-term planning. She gave up her newborn sons to aim for a significant future outcome.

"What happened to Rebecca is the exact reason why I don't want any more shootouts in the streets of New York," I announce. "Our mother lost everyone, literally everyone, and gave her life to avenge her family. And why? Because our fathers craved power. Everyone dies in the end. It's how we live our lives, no matter who we are, that makes all the difference. We'll annihilate the Slavs, and we'll create what we set out to create."

"Hear, hear!" Kai exclaims.

"Let's do it," Logan says.

Maisy shoots to her feet. "I want to help."

Logan cuts her off. "Absolutely not!"

"Over my dead body, baby girl." Kai grabs her by the hand and tugs. "Now sit your ass down."

She wrenches her hand away from Kai's and remains standing. "Why not? I was there, I know their operation. I also spent time with Milan. I know them better than anyone." She sits on my lap. "Orion, come on. Let me help," she pleads.

I don't want to be harsh with her, like Logan and Kai were. I smile, kiss her cheek, and tuck a few strands of her hair behind her ear.

"Maisy," I sigh, "this war, it's *ours*."

"I want to dance in its ashes too, Orion. If I'm part of your lives, you gotta allow me to contribute."

I glance over at Kai and Logan.

"Didn't you just hear me? Over my dead body, Orion," Kai repeats.

I agree with Kai, but we can't shut her out. "Logan?"

"I don't want her in the line of fire. And if she's helping, that's exactly where she'll be," Logan points out.

"It's because I'm a Slav, am I right?" she protests.

"No, Maisy. It's because you're our addiction, you're too precious to us, and we don't want you to get hurt." I turn to Logan and Kai. "But now that she's to be part of our lives, the dynamic of our relationship must change. And that means we let Maisy contribute. Especially when she has inside knowledge. The little fact that she's a genius could help, too."

"Goddamn!" Logan's clearly annoyed.

Kai sighs, looking frustrated. "I don't want her anywhere near the Slavs. Agree to that and I'm cool."

"One hundred percent." I turn to Maisy. "Did you hear? We don't want you out of this penthouse until the war is won. Clear?"

"Yes!" She smiles naughtily, as if we didn't just make a huge decision in our lives. None of us said it, but the moment I used the word *relationship*, we all felt it. Like the elephant in the room. She didn't seem to pick up on it, though, which is for the better. As for us, it's time to grow up.

"Tell us what you know," I tell her.

She goes back to the couch, crosses her legs beneath her, and regards us seriously, one by one.

"Right. What I know about them, and what I've seen, is that they win by numbers. It seems that they have too many Slavs on their books when they show up, but actually, they don't. They hire men to do their dirty work, then leverage the completed job against them by blackmailing them, threatening to kill their families, and the rest. You get the point."

"What you're saying is that these men are just unwilling accomplices? Stooges?"

"Exactly that. And if you dig deeper, you'll probably find that they don't really have anyone loyal to them, apart from maybe a few. And even the loyal ones,

Milan treated like crap. I'm sure Rosey is too. He never paid them any good. Apart from Zed. He was his right hand."

"The fucker!" Logan spits. He must be dwelling on the fact that Zed was the one who struck the final blow to our mother before she died. "I'm glad we were the ones who killed that motherfucker!"

"Me too!" Kai says.

I nod my agreement and glance at Maisy. "By the way, do you have any idea of what happened to her body?"

"Milan was cruel as fuck, but from what she said transpired between them, it sounded like he was really hurt, which tells me that he loved her. She could be buried somewhere in the grounds of the house. But that's just a theory."

"One that I intend to thoroughly check out when the time comes," I say. "Meanwhile, Maisy, you just gave me an idea on how to destroy the Slavs."

"Let's just kill them all," Logan growls.

Kai leans forward, his ears pricked up.

"Divide and conquer," I pronounce.

Kai frowns. He's not quite on board yet. "I need more details."

"You know I'd love to kill every Slav on this planet," I start. "Apart from Maisy, of course."

"Of course," Kai agrees, and Logan nods.

"Well, I'm thinking, why don't we give the men who are forced to work for the Slavs an option to leave? To relocate to a different city or state with their families."

Maisy's interest piques. "How?"

"And why not kill them?" Logan asks, seemingly unhappy with my idea.

"There are too many of them. If we start killing them, there'll be some kind of outcry and definitely an investigation. We can cover up five or ten bodies, even twenty, but a hundred? It's gonna be a logistical nightmare. What I suggest we do is approach them, one by one, with a get-out option. If they don't wanna do it, we kill them and deliver their bodies to the Slavs. This will scare them for sure. For those that wanna do it, we'll help them disappear."

"And how, may I ask, will you relocate hundreds of families?" Kai smirks, looking skeptical.

"Isn't that what the witness protection program does?" Maisy asks, ever the straight shooter.

"That's correct. All we need to do is find someone on the inside," I reason.

Logan isn't convinced. "And then what?"

"Actually, Logan, this might work," Maisy says. "People will do a lot out of fear. When the opportunity comes up and they see they could get themselves and their families away from this life, they might take up the offer."

"The witness protection program helps witnesses whose lives are in danger due to their cooperation with law enforcement," Logan points out.

"Yeah, that would be the catch," I say. "They'll have to agree to cooperate with the cops."

"Ha! Of course nobody will do it!" Kai scoffs.

"Those that haven't done the most heinous crimes would," Maisy responds, appearing to stifle a yawn. "For the others, they deserve to die anyway."

"Great. Just great." Logan is losing patience. "All you need now is a little thing called a U.S. Marshal and everything will be peaches."

"Yeah, that's a bummer." Kai rubs his chin sarcastically. "Do any of you happen to have someone on the inside?"

I don't need his sarcasm right now.

For some reason, Maisy raises her hand. "I do. It has been quite a while since I've spoken to him, but I do know someone from the U.S. Marshals Service. He runs the New York branch. Christopher Miller. I met him when my mother died, and again just before I turned eighteen," she starts, glancing between the three of us as she talks. "Back then I wondered why he talked to me, a nobody, but in a strange way, I trusted him. When I saw him at eighteen, he offered me a new life outside New York. He must have known more than he let on of course, but by then I lost interest in what he had to say.

I'd never leave my sister and he knew that." She rolls her eyes at the irony. "Silly me."

"When I said 'any of you' I meant Orion or Logan," Kai is quick to correct her. "Not you, baby girl."

Agreed. Her contribution so far is enough for sure. Yet, I can't seem to keep my mouth shut. "How well do you know this guy?"

Let's just explore all the options here. Who is this Christopher and what is he to her?

"Orion!" Kai warns me. *Me!* The fucker.

"Met him twice. So I don't know him at all. He seemed honest, and ambitious." She finally lets the yawn out and rests her head on Kai's shoulder. "I just couldn't imagine leaving Rosey behind."

"How tired are you, Maisy?" Logan asks her.

"Just a little." She closes her eyes as her head drops back to rest on the back of the couch. "But I'm fine here. I want to listen to you talk."

CHAPTER 10

KAI

Maisy must have been really tired to fall asleep on the couch.

While Logan tends to Uncle Jon, I scoop her up in my arms and take her to Orion's room. I'm not sure where I'll be sleeping but most likely it will be on the floor, next to Maisy. I don't fucking care what they say.

"Here we are, baby girl. You rest." I kiss her forehead and cover her with a sheet; I doubt she can hear me as she seems fast asleep.

I go back to the living room and for the first time, I fully take in Logan's penthouse and the luxury he lives in.

"She's fast asleep," I say, and sit down.

"In my room?"

"Yes."

"Good."

"Where will I sleep?" Now I'm just being polite.

"Fuck knows. I bet Logan has plenty of other rooms. Look at this place!"

"Yeah, that's not gonna cut it. I'm sleeping next to Maisy," I say bluntly.

Orion frowns. "Why d'you ask me then?"

I shrug. "I thought you'd offer."

"Fuck that. I ain't offering. I'm sleeping with Maisy."

"Fuck you, Orion. I'm sleeping next to Maisy, too. Do you know how much I suffered, how much I needed her, missed her?"

"Then where the fuck were you these two months?" he growls, finally confronting the unspoken. His voice is a mixture of anger and concern. His eyes blaze with intensity as they fix on me. "You didn't think *we* missed *you*? That we were worried over you?"

"Had I known Logan called in a hit on Maisy I'd have been here to kick his ass much sooner, I tell you that!" I try to avoid his penetrating stare. "Besides, I didn't think anyone would miss me."

"You didn't think?" Orion's words drip with incredulity and bitterness. "Do you have any idea how worried we've been? I missed you, damnit." His voice softens, betraying the vulnerability beneath his tough exterior. "You're not alone in this world, Kai. You've got family who care about you. And I'm not only talking about us being half-brothers."

"I'm sorry." I know I was an asshole, but I'll be goddamned if I'm taking all the blame.

"You should be. You wanna sleep next to Maisy? You're sleeping on the floor."

Yes! "I'll take that!"

Logan comes back just in time to catch the tail end of our conversation. "Floor? No way. I got a room for you, Kai, the best one!"

"Thanks, Logan, but no. I'll sleep next to Maisy, on the floor."

Logan looks at me, then at Orion, and breaks into laughter. "Is that how it's gonna be, huh? In my own penthouse? Should I sleep on the floor too?"

Orion's uninterested, just sipping at his whiskey. "Suit yourself."

"May I remind you that you already had her?"

A hint of a smile plays on Orion's lips. "And your point is?"

"Assholes. Both of you are assholes," Logan snickers, but deep down, we know he doesn't mind. Neither of us do.

"Mm-hmm. Now sit your ass down and let's talk about the Slavs. What do we think of this... Christopher Miller?"

"You're seriously set on doing this?" I ask.

"Do you have a better idea that doesn't involve a bloodbath?"

Logan and I look at each other. Nope. No other ideas. Especially now that Maisy's in the other room. I feel her magnetic pull drawing me to her, the source of my pain and desire. It's where I want to be. Not here.

"I didn't think so," he says after a long pause. Both of our minds must have wandered. At least, I know mine did.

"Let's pay him a visit." Logan has clearly been thinking with his mafia hat on. Unlike me. My cock is doing my thinking.

"Gotta take a piss, I'll be right back," I lie. I stand up and head down the corridor toward the room where I left Maisy. I want her so bad, my groin hurts, my balls ache, and my cock has been hard for the last four hours.

As I enter Orion's room, I hear Maisy's even breathing. She is my nirvana, and I'm taking what calms me: honey directly from her honeypot.

I sit on the bed next to her and hook my fingers into the waistband of her panties. I lift her ass to slide them off, leaving her with only her top on. Then I strip down to my boxers and throw everything on the floor. I need her skin. I need her scent. I need *her*. I sit between her legs, lifting one onto my shoulder, and start by kissing her ankle before making my way up to the apex of her thighs.

I'm taking my time, enjoying this woman who's taken all my reason, softly planting kisses on her inner thighs, heading toward her perfect crux. While with one hand I'm holding her leg, with the other, I gently stroke her thighs. It seems like she's sleeping, but I hear her sighing and notice her hips squirming a little. I stroke her everywhere apart from her silky folds.

Soon I reach the summit, and I cannot postpone the inevitable any longer. I hold her thighs open, hesitating a tad longer to build her anticipation of what's coming.

And there it is. Her tiny moan reaches my ears. She's restless, so I lean in and blow on her delicate skin, right up close.

"Are you ready for me, baby girl?" I inhale her scent and look up at her. Her sleepy eyes open, her eyelashes flutter, and she knows. Her eyes become hooded. She's not embarrassed; she even has a sly smirk for me.

"Kai…" she moans. "I'm always ready for you."

That's my green light. I press the flat of my tongue against her pussy, now soaked with arousal, and lick all the way up to her sweet nub.

This! This is what I've been craving all this time. She alters my mind. Art in its truest form. How is it possible that she tastes like a Michelin-star dessert, maybe even better?

And she needs me. *Me.* I push my tongue into her entrance, lapping up everything she has, holding her thighs firmly open, keeping her in place while she bucks against me, moaning as I continue to devour her swollen nub.

"Kai!" she breathes.

I pull back. "Yes, Maisy?"

"Kai, please." She raises her hips again and I wrap my forearm around the back of one of her thighs to keep her in place.

I lap up her juices and devour her cunt, my tongue swirling over her clit and sucking on that little fucker while I use my free hand to plunge two fingers inside her. Her thighs tremble and she treats me to a whimper, but I need a good, loud moan from her.

My fingers are coated in her juice. She moans as I take them out and swirl the arousal over her nub. Second thrust in and I'm deeper, to the knuckle, and I do this a few more times until she bucks and raises her hips into my fingers. I collect her arousal on my way out and rub it over her swollen clit some more. She lifts her head and looks at me with so much desire, I can tell she's ready.

I grin. "You like this, baby girl?"

She moans as I keep thrusting my fingers inside her and rubbing her nub, and I repeat the motion, over and over, until she throws her head back. "Kai!" she cries.

A rush of fluid dribbles out of her divine pussy. Her hips jerk up into my hand as she rides the waves of pleasure while her orgasm explodes through her body. She feels so fucking good.

I bring my soaked fingers to my lips and lick them. "The heavenly drink of the Gods, the liquid honey of the heavens... Fuck knows what else. All I know after this is that I'm high."

Maisy titters, and as I look up at her, her eyes land on someone behind me and I look around. I didn't hear Orion and Logan coming in at all.

Orion's eyes don't leave her. "Look at this little slut in my bed, Logan."

She giggles. She's ready to play, and so's my cock, who's aching by now.

Logan smirks. "I bet you she won't be able to walk in the morning. Come here," he orders her, pointing to the floor.

She hesitates for a moment but obeys him; wearing only her tiny top, she crawls off the bed on all fours and kneels, craning to look up at him. Fuck, that position is perfect, with her heels under her ass and her knees spread open. She's starved for a fucking. *And the way that ass sticks up in the air...*

Orion pipes up. "Take off my sweatpants and boxers."

With a smirk, she pulls down Orion's sweatpants and boxers in one, causing his freed cock to jut up. When they're fully off, he's stark naked.

"Now mine," Logan orders, taking his t-shirt off, and with Maisy stripping him from the waist down, he too is quickly buck-naked.

They want to fuck, but my cock has been straining in my boxers all this time. I remove my boxers too; my cock needs air. And Maisy, naturally. The moment it's out, I fist my hand around it and pump a few times, the precum glistening under the city lights streaming through the huge windows.

Orion strokes her cheek. "What we're gonna do tonight is fill you to the brim with our cum. Would you like that, Maisy?"

She gazes up at him and nods, wanton.

"Logan, pull out the bench and put it against the window. I want her to have the best view of the city as we fill her up."

I help Logan pull the bench out from under the bed, and we set it so it overlooks the city.

Still on all fours, Maisy crawls toward the bench and hunches over it. Her ass is raised up, her cunt glistening.

MAISY

"I haven't told you to move," Orion says coolly.

My mind is lost to them; what they do to my body and mind I can't explain. But around them, I'm carnal, unrestrained. They are the only men in my life who ever made me feel safe, and with them, I'm me. Maisy Roy.

I study him; his index finger is pointing to his feet. I crawl back to where I was, with Logan and Kai now standing behind me. Everyone's cock is hard, and I'm lost in all the desire. I don't wait. My fingers wrap around Orion's cock and I take over. With both hands I fist him, twisting at the base in a firm stroke, waiting for his ecstatic groan as I take him in my mouth. And there it is: Orion's head drops back and he releases an animalistic growl.

Kai kneels next to me and lifts my leg, shifting to lie under me on the floor and making me straddle him. As I do, Orion swings a foot over Kai's body to stand above him.

"Ride me, baby girl, to heaven and back," Kai says, and slides his cock inside my soaked pussy. I stifle a moan as his big cock expels the air from my lungs.

I blow Orion sloppily, utterly addicted to the groans that emerge with every bob of my head. Kai grabs a handful of my boobs and kneads them before pinching my nipples. Too much sensation is driving me crazy; I start riding him, my ass going into full twerking mode because I want to be able to draw ecstasy from every inch of these men.

"Oh, fuck... *Fuck!*" Kai groans.

Orion tangles his fingers in my hair and pulls me away. He lowers his lips to mine and devours my needy mouth. "Little fucking slut, you're just a toy to play with," he mumbles against my lips. "You hear me?"

I nod, and moan as he kisses me again. "Show me your tongue," he orders. I stick out my flattened tongue and he spits on it, then licks it, weaving our tongues together. The kind of pure, nasty filth that gets me off.

"Come on Orion, I need her, I need her ass." I hear Logan's voice and from the corner of my eye, I see him jerking off. "Sweetheart, the doctor needs his cum bucket."

Kai is banging me from below, having matched my rhythm of twerking, and Logan kneels behind me. He slaps my ass a few times, the sound reverberating around the room, and then I sense his finger moving over my sphincter and around the rim. The urge to buck against it is too strong. I ride Kai harder, addicted to every sensation they are offering.

When I look over my shoulder, Logan's fisting his cock. "You better be ready for me, 'cause I ain't stopping for nothing."

Kai slows down the pace while Logan pushes his finger into my ass, then pushes me down so he can get better access. Without any time to adjust I feel his cock at my ass, thrusting slowly, attempting to enter me. On the fourth try, his cock gains purchase and starts to stretch me out. It's too much fucking pleasure as my ass accommodates his girth, while Kai's cock continues to thrust from below; gradually, my body begins adapting to life in heaven.

I moan, loud; maybe I'm hoping God himself will hear me and I can tell him I never want to get off this ride.

"That's it, sweetheart, take it, take it like a big girl." Logan's fully inside, opening a gateway to paradise as he starts to fuck into me hard and rough, synchronizing his thrusts with Kai's. I feel every vein in his cock as I'm stretched out.

"Arrgh, you little cocksucking whore!" Kai cries as Logan digs his fingers into my flesh, holds my hips with both hands, and pounds me. He's big, but I find my rhythm and begin to move with them, bucking backward and forward, milking their cocks as if they're the last ones on earth.

Kai cups my breasts and squeezes my nipples between his fingers as Orion holds my head and resumes fucking my face, totally disregarding everything else my body is going through.

"Yes, yes!" I hear Orion groaning as I gag on his cock. My air intake is denied and I try to breathe while my body is ravaged by the pleasure patrol. Which, unbeknown to them, melts me down and, at the same time, makes me fly.

And when Kai reaches down and rubs my swollen clit, I explode, a burst of vibrant sensations igniting inside me, through me, as if I'm a burning fuse, releasing energy in the form of light.

In my head, a mesmerizing display of colors, shapes, and textures forms as I ride my own personal fireworks and skyrocket into a chaotic whirlwind of ecstasy.

Kai and Logan slow down and Orion allows me to gasp in a breath, though it sounds more like I'm howling.

Logan's lips are on my shoulder, peppering me with kisses, but he and Kai are still inside me, fucking me rhythmically, easing me into another orgasm while Kai tugs at my nipples and renders me unable to think straight.

But Orion's fingers tangle in my hair and he begins to tug me up, so I know this bliss is almost over.

"Brace yourself, sweetheart, I'm pulling out," Logan whispers, and as he does, I experience an instant aching for his body. Kai's too. I try to move down onto him again, but Orion won't let go of me.

ORION

Her pupils are dilated from the orgasm she just had. She's panting, lost to her high. And she wants more. She needs more, my sweet little slut.

I tug her up to me; her parted lips are all I focus on, and I slide my tongue alongside hers, breathing in her very being. I gotta control the animal awakened in me; I'm close to drawing blood from her lips.

"Remember how we bred you the last time?" I mumble into her mouth as my hand drops down to her breast.

She nods and presses into me as if she knows I'm craving her kiss, full of demonic promise.

"Without contraception, this is it. Now, you're gonna be a good little whore for us and let us fuck you and fill you with our cum."

Her eyes open but her pupils look unfocused; she's listening to me somewhere inside her head, and for a moment, I see the panic in her.

I glance over at Logan and Kai, who have got up and are now standing next to me. *Is this her nightmare?* They seem to notice the change in her too.

Before she can say anything, Logan pinches her chin and tilts her jaw toward him. He presses his lips to hers, claiming her mouth. I want her to get that she has no control over what we do. Because in a way, she's like a chess grandmaster, always three moves ahead.

"Who knows how many babies we'll put inside you," I whisper in her ear before biting her earlobe as Logan continues to kiss her.

She tries to pull back from Logan, set herself free from my fingers gripping her hair, but I'm not letting her go. Her scent is what keeps me glued to her, fucked, half-sated, like magic, and I want more. She's woken up a thousand devils inside me and they will not let go so easy.

Having sucked all the air out of her lungs, Logan pulls back, hooks his fingers under her top, and pulls it over her head. The material catches on her breasts a moment before they drop, abundant and bouncing in front of me. I'd love to put them in my mouth and suck on them, but in my head, she's bent over the bench on her tits and stomach, getting pounded and filled with our cum. For the time being, I knead them with both hands.

"O-Ryan…"

I love her like this, totally dazed from her own arousal, not knowing what's happening but understanding it's something she may not have agreed to.

"Now, lie face-down on that bench for us." I pinch her nipple hard and she bites her lip.

Kai's kneading her ass and her gaze shifts toward him, silently pleading for help. I know that look. She's not in control of what's happening, and it pushes her into unfamiliar territory.

Logan stands over the bench. "Over here, sweetheart."

Her gaze is fixed on Kai, then on me, before she silently makes her way over. Her dark eyes hold the whole universe inside them. Fear, panic, terror, but there's also lust there.

She reaches the bench and kneels over it, exposing her trained ass and glistening cunt, and fearfully watches Logan fist his cock in front of her face.

Her breasts just about reach the end of the bench as she's bent over it, not enough to hang over on the other side. But as much as I cannot stop thinking about them, tonight will be all about her ass and cunt.

As her ass lifts again, she moans. She's back where she was, in the neverland.

The three of us move to stand behind her and admire her spread legs, her ass and cunt open for us. She's not strapped to anything, and yet she knows to grip the bench with her fingers at either side.

"Perfection," Logan mutters, getting down on his knees. He slides his cock up and down her folds and she bucks backward, trying to get him in, in any hole.

"Oh, I know what you want," he laughs, and dips the head inside her cunt, then her ass. He alternates a few times, driving her crazy.

"Logan," she drawls, "fuck me."

I walk around the bench to look into her wanton eyes and pump myself. Upon seeing me, she raises her head and shows me her tongue. She's desperate to be face-fucked. I know what she wants, but she's not getting it.

"Whore," I say as she stares at me with overflowing lust and debauchery. *I love her.*

"Fuck it!" Logan gives in and plunges into her asshole like a crazed man on drugs. He digs his fingers into her hips and starts pounding her hard. Beastly grunts tear from his throat; he seems intent on expelling all the air from her lungs. Each thrust is going in to the hilt and out to the tip; she's feeling every vein, for sure. Her staccato moans tell me she's taking off and it's clear that it's working for Logan. He groans and takes his cock out as he spurts the first rope of cum, then slams into her cunt and continues filling her with the remaining jizz.

Logan slaps her ass and stands up. "I'll get the whiskey."

I position myself in the space he's vacated and kneel behind her. Kai's jerking his cock and staring longingly at Maisy, but I was faster.

I slap her ass cheek, and as she tilts it up for me I slap her right in the center, over her asshole. She makes a strangled sound as her arousal surges. She turns her head to gaze at me over her shoulder, her pupils still wanton and dilated. If she wanted to say anything, I know what it would be: *Finish me off.* I know any touch will go straight to her head and between her thighs. Her ass lifts higher still. *Little slut!*

She looks like she's losing it, not sure what to do with herself, so she lets go of the sides of the bench and, realizing there's nothing else for her to do, that this is where we want her, she grabs the top of the bench instead, squirming, waiting for me to start.

"Easy now. We gotta pace ourselves, and you gotta be able to hold our cum all night, my little whore. Easy. Just relax." I close in on her tight ass and slowly slide inside, making sure my piercing doesn't hurt her. But she's lost, bucking and shoving backward until she has me fully in. Every nerve in my body awakens; my cock has become a steel rod because this, right here, is where I want to die. In her ass. Pumping her full of cum.

"Yeah... Can you feel it?" I pull out, then thrust inside her again. "There. *Feel it.*"

"Yes, yes, yes... Yes, Orion," she moans.

"Goood girl." I pull out again, and thrust back in. Fuck me, she's so good. With every shove into her, she pushes me closer to ecstasy, but I don't want to go there yet. I want to be here, watching her beg for an orgasm. That's my heaven.

She reaches between her legs, tries to touch herself as she moans, but I immediately pull out. She gets it, and her hand goes back to holding the bench in front of her.

"You try that one more time and you're not getting anything tonight," I say, and slap her ass cheek.

She nods, and presses her forehead onto the bench, in frustration, I think. Still, her ass is tilted up again, and I just slide back in. The moment she's filled again she looks back at me, her mouth hanging open, and each time I pound her she lets out a deep moan. I love her like this, powerless, yet so intense she burns us to ashes with her power.

Logan comes back with a bottle and three glasses, placing them on the table by the door and proceeding to pour.

Maisy's whimpering. The way her eyes plead with me makes me want to reach between her legs just to watch her explode.

"Why're you looking at me?" I ask as I thrust to the hilt. "What do you want? *Say it.*" I slap her ass cheeks again.

"B-B-Breed me ..." she gasps. She thinks I'll cum and that she'll get to, too. *Ha. Funny.*

"Goddamn, you feel so good!" I growl, and ram into her. She whines loudly and jerks backward toward me; she's dangerously close, chasing her high in her subspace. I claw at her ass cheeks and spread her wider, allowing myself space to slam against her ass and push her harder onto my cock. I won't last long like this.

"Fuck, that's it, *fuck!*" I seize her by the shoulders, leveraging her body against my chaotic thrusts. "You want my cum, slut? Open that cunt of yours." I pull out of her ass and pound her cunt, continuing to ram through my peak, grunting loud as my cum fills her up, spurt by spurt, making her all sloppy and wet. She looks back at me, her eyes hooded and hungry, pleading for release, and gives me a drawn-out moan.

I could stay buried inside her all night. I could. But it's Kai's turn. He needs her, like we all do. At least now that she's ours, we can work on her all day, every day. I pull my cock out of her sloppy cunt, wipe it on her ass, and straighten up. Logan passes me a glass of whiskey, and we clink our glasses.

Kai leaves his untouched on the table. He's in a hurry. He gets on his knees behind her and strokes her back.

"K-Kai…" There's relief in her voice that it's him. He has a habit of yielding to her desires.

But even for him, seeing her ass stretched, he doesn't wait. He enters her deep, fully, and starts pumping. His fingers claw at her hips and he's grunting. All the while, arousal is dripping down her legs.

"I-I can't anymore. Please…" she pleads.

He accelerates the pounding as Maisy's body jerks on the bench with every stroke. She's whimpering; all her nerve endings must be screaming in her head.

"Oh, fuck!" he exclaims as his cock continues to slam inside her ass, and she starts to shake. But Kai knows the game; just as he orgasms, he pulls out and thrusts inside her cunt. We're creating the perfect cream pie for her, and he growls long as jizz fills her for a third time.

"Kai, Kai, Kai… No, no!" she begs; she's been on the verge of heaven all this time. She's sticky and leaking as she lies on the bench, her ass tilted up, her asshole spasming.

I finish the whiskey and set the glass back on the table, then go and pick Maisy up from the bench and put her on the bed.

My room in Logan's penthouse has a king-size bed, which would probably fit three of us, but not four. The fourth one will be sleeping on the floor.

Logan pours us another drink and hands us the glasses. We clink and drink in silence.

Only Maisy's whimpers can be heard. "Please... I need to cum..."

"Not yet, darling. I want you to lie on your back now," I say softly. "We don't want all that cum to leak out, do we?"

"Y-You're serious?" She sounds terrified, but pants as if she needs to be fucked some more.

"Why would I want to breed you if I wasn't serious?"

"But... I thought... Fuck, I can't think straight right now." She puts her hand between her legs and starts rubbing herself.

"Sweetheart, no." Logan takes her hand away and kisses it.

"Do something, please... I need you! All of you! Please!"

Logan's ready to go again so he maneuvers between her legs, and Kai and I get on either side of her on the bed. He brushes his cock against her sticky cunt, going up and down her folds, and as he enters her, she whimpers.

I grab one of her legs under the knee and pull it up and out. Kai does the same with her other leg. This opens and raises her cunt higher, and will allow for more cum to enter her.

"Yesss!" Logan's above her, one hand on either side of her body as he pounds her to the hilt; the rhythm he is building makes her whine with pleasure. Her soft fingers wrap around my cock and she starts pumping with a heavenly stroke, and I see she needs more when she fully takes me in her mouth.

Logan tries to slow down, but she doesn't let him. She bucks upward, milking his cock as if it's the last one on earth, and his driving force ramps up to match hers. He starts to lose it; I would too if I had her wide open like this, being filled with my cum.

Her other hand is wrapped around Kai's cock; she never forgets any of us when we play, and he reciprocates eagerly. He pinches her nipples as her tits bounce and jiggle between us.

Logan's picking up speed, making her whole body vibrate. He pounds her into oblivion and growls as he ejaculates, emptying his balls for the second time into her sweet, hot cunt.

I'm close; her sucking skills are out of this world, and she seems happy so long as she has my cock in her mouth. The way she works her tongue under my cock, and the way she squeezes my balls, I'm literally holding off with each second. But I will not be getting her to swallow today.

Logan pulls out of her, exhausted.

"Hold her legs." I make my way between them, cock in hand, and growl as the first rope escapes me and lands on her pussy, but the rest I make sure I get inside, as she's held open for me. I empty each last drop into her sweet, sticky, celestial well.

"Fuck me... You're one helluva cock-sucking, breeding whore, Maisy!" I cry out in my excitement.

Kai leans down, sucking her nipples, tugging on them as she chases her high, still not being allowed to cum.

"Let me blow you, Kai, please," she pants.

Kai grins and releases her leg, straightens up, and pushes his cock into her mouth. Logan drops her other leg and collapses onto the bed next to her. Maisy squeezes Kai's balls as she sucks his cock deep, hungry. *This is the slut I love. Always craving cock.*

She bobs her head, lapping him up as he tangles his fingers in her hair and picks up the pace, fucking her mouth, harder and harder, his grunts louder each time, pulling her flush against his groin. The wet pops of her mouth are the only thing I hear, along with her stifled moans.

I sit between her legs, admiring the view of her workout. At her side, Logan does the same.

She is divine like this, starved and hungry for sex. I don't think I ever want to allow her to cum.

"Move, O-Ryon!" Kai shouts, just before I get totally carried away by watching her.

She's nursed him to orgasm fast. I get off the bed and he sits where I was. He pushes her knees open and enters her as he orgasms, his grunts telling me his load is big. *Perfect*.

CHAPTER 11

LOGAN

Desperate, her eyes jumped from me to Kai to Orion throughout the night. Like a woman on drugs, trying to guess who had her next hit.

We made sure she didn't orgasm. And we couldn't get enough of her. Halfway through the rowdy night, she collapsed onto the bed, falling asleep pretty quickly.

Lying naked between us, she was perfect. We all found a place on the bed around her; me on one side, Kai on the other, and Orion sprawled across the foot of the bed.

We stayed up until late, talking. Trying to make sense of what Maisy had told us, trying to remember any other clues about our mother. It is still a shock, one that will not go away just like that. Also, where was she buried? How did they dispose of her body?

I've been pretty much disassociated from my emotions, but deep down, I know all I've been doing is searching for my mother.

I missed her in my life. I did. And I learned to hide my emotions well because they'd crucify me. How could the son of Lorenzo *cry*? Or ask for Mommy? I was aching, not only for a mother, but for a normal childhood. Which I never got. None of us did. Well, maybe Kai did. I dunno. I just know that every step I took, I hoped there would be a sign of her, a trace of the woman who had given birth to me.

I was hung up on her for years and now that she exists as a reality in my mind, I'm angry that I never got to meet her. All because of Milan. Maisy was right to kill him.

Another subject came up. What about tonight? Without her implant, she could get pregnant. The chances would be very low as I only just got that last piece of the implant out, but I know how it works. Nothing's certain when it comes to pregnancy. And with so much cum in her cunt, I wouldn't be surprised if she conceived. *Do we want that?*

We talked seriously about the consequences of our sex fest, but none of us thought it probable that she'd conceive. This is the game she loves. So, no harm done.

Are we ready to get her pregnant? No. We haven't had enough of her yet and if that happened, she would get it dealt with, so we said no more on the subject. The three of us agreed on it. Babies in our world are not allowed.

When it was time to sleep, Orion made us leave the bed, even though there was enough space for two of us plus Maisy. I ended up sleeping on the floor – in my own penthouse.

I didn't care, though. I took the sheets and pillow from my room, got some for Kai, and we slept on either side of the bed.

Orion's the biggest asshole when it comes to Maisy. We know that, and yet we haven't said anything. We also know that Orion's always put us before him for most of our lives, and now that he's not anymore, we've silently agreed that we'll endure it.

I want to see Orion happy.

Just like I am, this very moment.

It's dawn already and we've hardly slept, except Maisy, who's been sleeping for six or seven hours. And for all those hours, she's probably been dreaming of sex. Actually, she *must* have been dreaming of sex because sweet, soft moans wake me up, and upon opening my eyes, I see her riding Orion's cock on the bed. I'm not sure if Orion is awake or not, but I know that his cock must be hard because she's dancing on him in slow motion, like a slowed-down bucking bronco. And seeing her bringing herself to orgasm is seriously the best sight ever. She whimpers sweetly, grinding faster and faster on his rod, and I hear them both reach their orgasm.

And then my sweet Maisy climbs off the bed, crawls along the floor to me, and does exactly the same thing. Without saying a word, she rolls me onto my back, and of course, my cock is hard and weeping with precum thanks to the show I just watched. She gets on top of me and rides me to heaven and back, taking me with her, giving me the world. My hands rest on her thighs and she reaches her peak again as she twists, wriggles, and sways to her own rhythm, faster and faster. I cum hard and fast, in a whole new way, while she's chasing the light she pushed me to.

Like a ghost in the night, Maisy leaves me and finds Kai on the other side of the bed. I can't see them, but I know what's happening. I hear Kai's groans while she gets yet another orgasm, something promised to her last night but never given. So this morning, she's taking everything from us. She's taking the control back. *Clever Maisy.*

"We need coffee." Orion's gravelly voice is extra deep in the morning.

"I'll get it," Maisy sing-songs, jumping up to her feet. When she moves to the foot of the bed I see her: her breasts heavy, her nipples pink, pebbled, beautiful, and her rosy cheeks hinting at the licentious deeds of the night we've had.

"Isn't it too early?" Kai mumbles.

"You don't have to wake up. I have some unfinished business with Maisy." Orion props himself up on his elbows and snickers. "It appears that she took something without asking."

She grins and stalks out of the room buck naked. "Coffee's on the way."

MAISY

After a night I will never forget, if only because they left me wanting them more than I could ever have imagined, I woke up safe, sated, and surrounded by my men. But the moment I opened my eyes, I took what was mine. Logan and Kai, they were way too happy, but Orion wasn't. He hates me for topping from the bottom. Still, I got my orgasm. Three, to be precise.

But this morning, I have the tiniest niggle in my head, reminding me that without contraception, any silly play could get me pregnant. My only comfort comes from the fact that I haven't had my period yet, even though Logan says I could get pregnant before my period comes. I should be careful. Or talk to Logan about having another implant inserted.

Offering to make coffee left me having to fend for myself in Logan's kitchen, but I managed to mock something up. I'm not sure the coffee I made will actually be any good.

In any case, I take four cups of the steaming, fresh brew and go back to Orion's room. Leaving the tray on the table, I pick up my cup and go back to bed.

Orion's eyes are open. He's watching me as I fluff my pillow and make myself comfortable.

I offer him my cup. "Want some?"

He reaches out and our fingers brush, sending shivers down my spine. This morning feels different. Unlike any other time. First, we're not at Orion's, so this is new, and second, I feel them closer, more intimate. Mine. A web of desire from which there is no escape has been cast over me, and I love it.

Orion sits up and nearly finishes my coffee. "Thanks. I needed that."

I frown. "I only offered you a sip. Not the whole cup."

"I'll get you a fresh one, darling." He kisses my cheek. "Only the best for you."

"I was joking. Come to bed, Orion." I try to grab him before he moves out of my reach.

"I need to get my laptop anyway." He playfully kicks Logan, who's now lying at the base of the bed.

"Mmm... yes. Coffee," Logan croaks.

Kai's on the floor, on my side of the bed, and I nudge him with my foot, hoping to get him up. But I'm unsuccessful. He takes my foot in his hands, kisses it, and places it under his cheek, making himself comfortable. I try to pull it back, but he holds it tight and starts tickling me.

"Kai!" Involuntarily, I kick him right on the nose.

"Ouch!" he cries.

"Oh, God, sorry, Kai! I didn't mean to hurt you. You had my foot–"

"Ignore him. He deserved that." Orion walks in with another cup of coffee, plus his laptop tucked under his arm. He passes me the cup and takes one for himself from the tray.

"Your coffee's here," he tells Kai and Logan, and sits next to me on the bed. The glow of his laptop screen illuminates his face as he opens it up. "What was the name of that U.S. Marshal again? Christopher... what?" he asks.

"Miller. Christopher Miller."

His fingers dance across the keyboard, and he weaves through layers of encrypted data until he unearths a dossier on Christopher. It says his name right there: *C. Miller, U.S. Marshal.*

As the data from Christopher's file becomes clear, Orion's gaze hardens. He peruses the documented details of Christopher's career, his family ties, and basically, his entire life. Then, his lips curl into a sardonic smile.

"What? What did you find?" I ask.

"He appears to be a beacon of righteousness," Orion hums.

"What else?" Kai asks as he sits on the bed. Everyone looks to be intrigued by Orion's findings.

"That's it. In a world full of darkness, he appears to be an angel."

Logan takes both cups of coffee, passes one to Kai, and sits on the bed too. "Bullshit."

"I agree. But it's all there. Clean as a whistle, at least on paper. And if he isn't, we'll know when we see him."

"Right," Kai agrees.

"How we gonna go about it?" I ask.

"This is your contact. I think you should meet him," Orion suggests. "Before we pay him a visit."

"Are you crazy?" Logan snaps at him.

Orion's on my side. For once. "Logan, Maisy can stand her ground. Give her the benefit of the doubt."

Kai voices his concern too. "Yeah, I'm not sure about it."

"It's not like we're gonna let her go by herself. We'll be there, too," Orion argues.

"Yeah, we sure as hell will be," Logan says through gritted teeth.

"I haven't seen him in years," I remind them. "What if he doesn't remember me?"

"I'll email him, in your name. If he remembers you, we'll set up a meeting," Orion decides. "If he doesn't, we'll pay him a visit."

~

The four of us have been staying at Logan's for the last two weeks. From the moment I got here, Kai didn't want to go back home. And Orion, of course, was recuperating, although I know all of us wanted to be together. Uncle Jon is not exactly the happiest he's ever been, Logan says. But I love it. I feel like a princess in the high tower, protected by my knights. Well, they're more like angry, sexy men, but I'll take what I can.

And the plan has been going ahead. In the last week, Orion has managed to set up a meeting with Christopher Miller. Considering how many years have passed, I was surprised that he remembered me.

And I actually met him two days ago. I won't forget the tension crackling in the air like static as Logan and Kai watched from afar, concealed in the shadows outside the restaurant I was in, their gaze never wavering. I felt it. Orion had to keep a closer eye on me, and so he was inside the restaurant, two tables on my left.

As for the meeting, I wasn't sure I'd remember Christopher. I was a bit apprehensive but the moment I saw him, I recognized his smile – totally disarming. He's in his forties, and still striking with his impressive height and build. His salt-and-pepper hair only adds to his appeal. But he seemed okay; I saw him as nothing but someone who could be quite helpful to our plan. Although, there was a moment when his eyes lingered a tad too long on my chest, but maybe I was mistaken.

The more I talked to Christopher, the more I realized he knew quite a lot. He knew things about me that I had only recently discovered. More specifically, he knew I was a Slav. Apparently, he knew all this time. Hence the reason why he wanted to help me back then. In fact, he was glad I'd made contact with him.

That was when I realized I had to improvise. I got him to believe that now, as one of the Slavs, I'm taking charge, and I want the Slavs disbanded. Would he help me do this? Because I, as a Slav myself, did not want to be part of the mafia and I wanted to try to relocate everyone in the Slav family, if that was possible. To allow Rosey and myself to have a good life. Like my mother wanted for us.

He couldn't give me an answer immediately. He for sure knew something else was at play, but why would he care if this would give him the access he needed to meet, record, and relocate all the Slav members in New

York? This was his moment to shine in front of his bosses. He was working under the Department of Justice at the end of the day.

As soon as he said he couldn't give me an answer, Kai was outside the restaurant within a minute. Wearing his helmet, biking leathers, boots, and gloves, he revved his bike and motioned with his head for me to come out. I had to excuse myself, and I left in a hurry. Although, Christopher had enough time to tell me that he'd come back to me soon.

CHAPTER 12

KAI

Out of the three of us, Orion's the one who would hold his horses down until a deal was done. He can control his emotions when needed. As for me, I'm a lost cause. I didn't think I was a jealous person at all until I saw Maisy talking to Christopher Miller. She had a hidden mike on her, and Logan and I used binoculars to watch her closely, and, everything was fine until he looked at her tits. *Our* tits. I saw through his façade and recognized him for who he truly was, a man with lecherous intentions. And that wasn't my emotions ruling my brain. Every gesture he made dripped with deviousness, a concoction most likely designed to ensnare Maisy. Or fuck her. One of the two.

And for someone so smart, I hate that she was unaware of the danger that lurked beneath Christopher's charismatic veneer. At one point she leaned in close to him, her laughter so pure I bet he thought he stood a chance. All the while, my heart twisted with anguish, and my knuckles were white with suppressed rage. And when he told her he couldn't give her an answer today, it was clear any more time spent with him was of no use to us.

"I'm getting her," I grumbled to Logan. I revved up my bike and rode over to the restaurant. No one stopped me. Orion must've heard me via his earpiece but said nothing, and Logan probably agreed with me.

It wasn't rehearsed, but once Maisy heard me, she stood up. She said her goodbyes and hurried out to meet me. There weren't any words exchanged between us; I just handed her the helmet and she climbed on the bike.

Orion and Logan met us at the penthouse. Sitting on the couch, back in their three-piece-suit attire after months of wearing sweatpants, they looked like the menacing mafia heads they are. But no matter what we wore, whether leather biker gear or an impeccable suit, our thoughts were the same.

Maisy's naïve voice filled the room, breaking the silence. "That went well, don't you think?"

Orion's eyes narrowed. "It did? How so?"

"Um, well, he couldn't give me an answer immediately, but I knew that would happen. He'll have to go and talk to his boss."

Orion and Logan looked at each other. Maisy held her ground, but I thought we'd all go crazy if she had to talk to him again.

Logan was about to lose it. "I say we kill him, he already knows too much. He knew you were a Slav all this time. That in itself warrants a kill. He betrayed you. In our world, if you really were a mafia head, you'd kill him now. And really, you are."

"Whoa. Easy, Logan," Maisy smirked. "We won't kill him just yet. We'll stick to the plan and see if it works." She looked to Orion for support, but the way his nostrils flared as he inhaled was a dead giveaway. She shrugged. "Yes, the fact that he knew I was a Slav really threw me off, he could have told me all those years ago. Why do you think he didn't?"

"It's his damn job. He probably knows us too." I retort with anger.

She nodded, but did not waver. "We stick to the plan. Orion?"

Orion nodded, although begrudgingly. "Maisy's right. Let's see if this will work out."

At that moment, the cell we got for Maisy, which realistically was for us because she didn't really want it, pinged with a message. Orion read the message out loud.

"Dearest Maisy, it was great seeing you after all these years. I note that you've grown into a beautiful woman. It was a pleasure talking to you. As a follow-

up, I wanted to say that I fully support you in dismantling the Slavs. I called my boss immediately and after confirming with him, I'm happy to help you. Let me know the details."

"Perfect." Orion's eyes moved to us, then back to Maisy. "We're starting tonight."

That very night, while I was having the most amazing, jealousy-fueled sex, our men were sent to find one Slav and offer him a relocation.

Of course, once they found him, we were told afterward, he wouldn't hear of it, and as per our plan, he was killed and thrown on the lawn outside the Slavs' house with a message on his chest: *Leave, or die.*

A few days later, when our men got the next Slav, it was the same story, and he too ended up dead on the Slavs' lawn.

It was after ten days that we made the first breakthrough. The Slav our men got wanted to relocate, to start a new life, and he was happy to bring his family. Orion texted Christopher from Maisy's cell and it was that very evening that he got picked up.

Orion's plan was crazy, but it worked. It's been four weeks now, and each week we relocate someone. A few Slavs have come forward, talked to Christopher themselves. It's funny how nobody wants to be part of the mafia if there's a way out. I wonder if this would have been the case with the Delgados. Would they want to be relocated if they were given the chance? Thinking like that gets me paranoid.

So many Slavs we sent away, and all this time, Christopher thinks he's communicating with Maisy on her cell.

The plan's shaping up pretty good; we haven't lost any of our men, though we're still staying in Logan's penthouse, having made Logan's Uncle Jon move into one of the apartments below. We've taken over the whole floor. Maisy's been given a room, too. And she loves it. Orion had Maisy's bed brought from his house to her room in the penthouse. We love it. The four of us sleep in her bed every night.

The way it's heading, there won't be any more Slavs to kill if we were to start a war now. Orion's plan is really working.

And now, with the weather getting hotter, and Maisy's clothing getting skimpier by the day, we're all spending our free time on the roof deck when we can. Work is taking over; there isn't only one plan in action.

Each of us is working with our families on the idea of joining forces. We want to have the majority on board before we give them the news – that we are family already.

And this takes us away from here, from Maisy. Which she hates.

I look up and see her sunbathing in the late sun; the gold bikini she wears is a winner. She chose it herself from a catalog. She knows it accentuates the best parts of her body. Orion, Logan, and I are under shadow on the roof deck, on our laptops, sending emails, working, and making sure every branch within our family is checked, counted, and double counted. We will not leave one stone unturned this time. Orion's single-mindedness has reached unprecedented levels.

The sound of a message pings, and I reach for my cell to check if it's mine. Once I realize it's not, I look up to see Orion and Logan staring at Maisy's cell. This is the cell that Orion looks after, the one we use to communicate with Christopher. It's lying on the table. The ping of the message sounds again.

"What does he want?" I ask.

Orion picks it up and reads the message aloud. *"Maisy, I'll probably get promoted next month, and it would be my honor if you'd allow me to take you to dinner."*

"Aw, that's sweet," Maisy says, not moving a muscle from where she's lying in the sun.

"No," Logan says bluntly, and continues working on his laptop.

"Abso-fucking-lutely no way," I say and look at Orion, waiting on his opinion, which I know will concur with ours.

Maisy raises her head and looks our way with her hand over her eyes.

"I agree," Orion says. "Christopher wants to fuck you. It's obvious."

Maisy sits up and puts her shades on to get a better look at us. "Christopher is a middle-aged man! He does not want to *fuck* me, thank you very much! He's just grateful."

"Maisy." Orion gives her a reprimanding look.

"I want to go to dinner," she pouts. "You three have never thought to take me out to dinner all this time, and I'm a woman. I want to be wined and dined."

"What?!" Logan gapes at her. "We wine and dine you every night. Not outside, but in here, you're our queen! And we treat you like one!"

"I want to be your queen outside, too."

"Is that what you want? For us to take you to dinner?" Orion asks.

"Yes," she says. "I'd like that."

"You know we said until we deal with everything that's a potential danger to you, you won't be leaving the tower, right?" Orion starts. "And you know that in the last few weeks we've had people, Slavs in particular, trying to get to you here, yeah? That damn sister of yours just doesn't give up!"

Orion's referring to the few occasions when the Slavs tried to take Maisy back. Lucky for us we were ready, and expecting them.

"Yes, I know, but–"

"There's no but. You're not going to dinner. At least, not with Christopher Miller."

Orion responds to Christopher's text, then reads it out loud. *"Thank you for the offer, but I'm going to decline. Maisy."*

I honestly don't get why they don't want me to meet Christopher. I don't think he wants to fuck me. What he's doing is too important for him to mess up our relationship.

MAISY

I usually spend my mornings on the roof deck in my panties and cami top. I have privacy plus all the space I need, and I'm free. When I came up here on my own for the first time, it was hilarious. That morning, the boys woke up and panicked, thinking I was gone. But soon, they learned: if I'm not down there, I'm here.

This morning, though, I know the three of them were awake as I left. For the first time since I've been with them, I rejected their advances.

I really wanted to go to the dinner Christopher invited me to. And I'm upset. Mostly about the way they told me no. I've been cooped up here, and yes, I know it's for my own safety, but once in a blue moon, I'd love to go out. And this was a perfect opportunity.

True, perhaps I've been lulled into a false sense of safety, but still, I wish they'd say they'll take me out to dinner after all this is over.

I want to be paraded as theirs. I want to show them off as mine. I want... I just want to be free, and go out like a normal person.

I sigh and tilt my head back to look up at the sky. It soothes me. The sun, the fresh air, the clear blue sky, everything seems perfect.

Suddenly, the ping of a message sounds from somewhere. I look around; nobody else is on the roof deck. On the table, under the shade, is a cell phone. One of the boys must have left theirs here, or maybe... I stand up to grab it. This is *my* cell. Well, they got it for me, but I don't really need it. Who am I going to call, anyway? Rosey? She showed me her true colors when she sent her people to take me. I still don't get her. There must be something that I'm not seeing, because to have her turn against me like that, her own sister, is outrageous – and heartbreaking. All this can't just be over power.

I flip the cell over, and there on the screen is a message from Christopher. It wouldn't hurt if I read it. It's my cell, after all.

"Your sister, Rosey, contacted me. She wants to relocate. And she wants you to meet her children before she goes. Let me know what you want to do."

Rosey? She wants to relocate? How did she find out about this?

"Are you texting someone?"

Orion's voice startles me; I let out a shriek and the cell slips from my hand.

"Orion! You scared me!" I spin around to face him. He's naked bar his boxer shorts and his hair's disheveled. He must have just got out of bed.

He picks up the cell from the floor. "As far as I remember, you got no one to text or call." He eyes me suspiciously. "Right?"

"I got a message from Christopher," I say, and hold my breath.

He checks the cell. "Did you respond?"

"I was gonna."

Orion looks over the message and judging by his face, particularly his big frown, he's not happy. "Please tell me you didn't consider it. Tell me you saw it's a trap!"

I frown. "Um, I don't think it is."

Orion looks enraged. "*Your-sister-kidnapped-you*," he hisses through gritted teeth. "She paid a million dollars for you and kept you in isolation, waiting on you to get your period so they could all rape you. You got away in the nick of time. What makes you think she's telling the truth? And Christopher, for that matter?"

"Because, well, he knows that all I wanted to do back then was to help my sister. Why should this be any different?"

"Because he works with your sister, maybe? Goddamn, Maisy, if I didn't know you any better, I'd think you were the most gullible person in the world."

"I see this could be a trap, but what if it isn't?" I counter. "This is my chance to meet my nephews and niece. My family. I thought for a long time I had no one in this world except for Rosey, but not anymore. And as much as I hate her and everything she's done to me, I don't want to miss out on this one chance. Even at the cost of my own freedom."

"She will kidnap you, *again!*" he yells. "And this time, maybe we won't come to save you. I've had enough of being shot at because of you! If that happens, do not count on me!"

"Oh yeah? Last I checked, you didn't save me from the Slavs!" I shout back at him. "I saved myself!"

"And the other times? For fuck's sake, Maisy, your reckless decisions would kill me one day. My body needs to recover and regain strength before you try something stupid again!" he bellows, his lips curling into a snarl.

Kai shows up on the roof deck, holding a cup of coffee. "We can hear you perfectly fine, Orion. No need to yell." He too is wearing nothing but boxer shorts. He settles under the shade. "What's going on?"

"The head of the Slavs, as she calls herself, is offering her children up as bait to try to get Maisy out of here!" Orion rages. He turns to Kai and shows him my cell. "Read for yourself."

Kai reads it, then looks at me. "The fuck? Come on, baby girl. You're smart enough to see it for yourself. Right?" He takes the phone from Orion and as he starts to type, recites, *"Hi, Christopher, that's not a good idea. Maisy."* He looks pointedly at me. "And, send."

"Kai! *I* wanted to respond! I mean, what if... What if I get her to come here?"

"No!" both of them reply in unison.

"Give me my cell!" I hold out my hand. Kai looks at Orion, who nods.

I take it and start typing, but then delete what I write, and again, I try to type. I'm not sure what to say, but I want to say *something*. They're not gonna take my voice away.

"What are you gonna say?" Kai asks.

I read out loud as I type. "*However, I'd like to meet up for lunch if the offer still stands. Today. Maisy.*" I look at Orion. Under the sun, he looks like a black hole that swallows everything in its path. "Send," I add, and smile inwardly. I dare not show on the outside how satisfying that was.

Orion is not letting up. "Why? Why do you want to expose yourself to danger? They want to draw you out of here, and now, they've succeeded."

"You think everyone's bad, don't you?" I retort. "Christopher's on our side. And this will give me a chance to ask him about Rosey, and her children."

"Really? Does he know you're staying at the Vitali penthouse? Riding on a Delgado bike, fucking a Carte?" he barks at me. "Because if he did, you'd be the first to be interrogated!"

He storms away from the roof deck like a hurricane.

Kai's shaking his head at me. "He's right. You're putting not only yourself in danger, but us too." He too turns to leave, then stops and regards me with poignant intensity. "You know, one of these days, something's gonna happen and we'll be gone. We *are* going to die for you, literally."

"Live for me instead, Kai. That's all I want."

Kai hangs his head sadly and leaves me, too. The win I had a moment ago now tastes bitter in my mouth.

But another ping of my cell draws my attention away from my dejection.

"Of course. Meet me at one o'clock at Avra Madison. It's on the corner of 60th and Madison. Christopher."

"See you then," I text in reply, then settle in my chair, soaking up the sun. I cannot wait to get out of this place.

Logan's voice startles me. "What was all that commotion, so early in the day?"

I only glance at him. There's nothing to say.

They don't understand the connection twins can have.

CHAPTER 13

MAISY

Orion did not get involved in preparing me like he did last time when I was meeting Christopher. There wasn't much time for me to get ready anyway, only a few hours, but Logan and Kai did all the work, albeit reluctantly.

They set up the miniature mic in the top button of my shirt, which right now is getting really tight around my neck and chest. Even my jeans are too tight on me, constricting my movements.

Maybe there is a danger for me out there from Rosey, but after all, I agreed to meet Christopher, not her. I know she despises me – she said so herself, she couldn't wait for me to get what she's gotten all these years – but somehow, deep down, I don't know... She's my sister, my *twin* sister. And ultimately, she needs me.

Kai's in his leather biker gear, including the helmet, so no one will recognize him. He drops me off at the restaurant, takes my helmet, and drives off into the distance, leaving me totally alone. I know I'm not truly alone; the three of them guard me with their lives all the time. And today is no different. Even Orion – he can act however he wants but I know he's in the background, watching over me.

I approach Avra Madison, and a hostess holds the door open for me. The restaurant is busy, but in an odd way, it makes me that much warier. I scan the tables in search of Christopher.

"Excuse me, do you have a reservation?" the hostess asks me as my gaze travels from table to table.

"Um, yes. I think so. Christopher Miller."

"And you are?" she probes.

"Maisy Roy."

I notice the hostess exchanging a glance with the man behind her, presumably the manager.

"Ah, yes. He's expecting you."

The moment I hear that, I feel relieved. Thank God. I got carried away in my scary thoughts, all because of Orion.

"Right this way, ma'am."

She leads me through the restaurant, and I notice that as I pass every second table, a person stands up and walks behind me. *Perhaps the restrooms are in the same direction?*

The realization that this could really be a trap becomes more vivid as we go deeper into the restaurant. I'm sure Kai told me about the exit routes, but I don't remember anything now. All this, slowly and surely, weighs on me like a heavy rock – this uncomfortable and terrifying feeling that I shouldn't have trusted Christopher.

Orion was right. Everyone was right.

The deeper we go into the restaurant, the darker it gets. *How come the lights are dimmed for lunch? Stupid, stupid Maisy.*

"Is there a private room that we're going to? We've passed through the whole restaurant," I ask the hostess, but really, I'm talking to Orion, Logan, and Kai through my mic. I need them to know where I am.

She doesn't respond but finally I see him, at the end of the wide corridor, sitting at the only table in here, right by the door with the green 'exit' sign lit above it. He's dressed in smart-casual, but all black, looking and feeling different from the last time I saw him. Last time, there was a genuine curiosity about me on his face. But now, everything's odd.

Christopher waves at me, his gaze soft but calculating as he watches me approach. Nothing's happened yet, and I remind myself that this is just a lunch. *But why am I feeling so uneasy?*

The fear of ending up alone in the basement at the Slav headquarters makes my heart pound in my chest, but I keep walking. Surely he didn't sell me out? Surely he's still the clean U.S. Marshal I met all those years ago? *Isn't he?*

Too late to turn back now. I'm gonna show Orion this will go like I said it would. Without any problems.

Christopher stands up as I approach. "Maisy, hope you're doing good."

I smile nervously as he gestures for me to take a seat across from him. "Please, sit down." I can feel how forced my demeanor is, but I try to ignore the knot tightening in my stomach.

"Christopher, it's good to see you," I reply, my voice trembling slightly.

I can't shake the feeling that something's terribly wrong. It's in the air. But before I can voice my concerns, Christopher nods toward the exit door on his left and my blood runs cold.

"Maisy, I'm really sorry for this," he says, "but I had no other option."

"Wh-What's going on?" I haven't even sat down fully before I'm upright again. Alert to the danger.

The police enter calmly, and men in uniform line up along the wall, their eyes all fixed on me. The men from the restaurant, the ones who followed me, do the same, all of them forming a circle around me. Panic grips me before I realize what's happening.

Guilt laces Christopher's voice. "I didn't believe Rosey when she showed me the video as it was grainy, but then she told me she has the gun as evidence, and I was left with no choice."

"What are you talking about?" I struggle to breathe, suddenly overwhelmed by nausea, and start to retch. But nothing comes up. There's just the sound of me heaving. *Surely Kai can hear me?*

Christopher glances at the closest man in uniform, who takes a step toward me.

"Maisy Roy Slavinovich, I'm arresting you on suspicion of the murder of Natasha Wilson. You have the right to remain silent. Anything you say, can and will be used against you in a court of law. You have the right to an attorney. If you cannot afford an attorney, one will be provided for you. Do you understand the rights I have just read to you?"

His voice becomes a distant murmur as he snaps the handcuffs onto my wrists, and my world crumbles around me. Once again, I am alone and helpless, with no hope of return.

"Natasha... who? M-Murder? I haven't killed any..." I retch again as I realize who they are talking about. Milan must have had cameras in and around the house. Rosey must have found the tapes. Rosey. Of all people, she was the one to betray me.

I peer toward the exit, searching for Orion, Logan, or Kai, but they're not there. "Save me," I whisper, "please…" They can hear me, I know they can.

Tears sting my eyes. I hope to God the police are mistaken but then again, they mentioned Natasha's name. I can't deny it. Even though she deserved it. I actually killed someone, and stupidly left the gun next to the body. Now I'm about to spend a lifetime in prison.

Christopher leaps up onto his feet and they lead me out of the restaurant through the back exit. A black limousine with blackout windows is parked across the road, and the back window slides down for a brief moment to reveal Rosey's face, twisted with satisfaction, before the window winds up again. *How could she have done this?* Does she hate me that much? Stupid Maisy. Being involved with the mafia, where else would I have ended up? Either dead in a ditch, being a hooker paid in heroin, or in jail. Stupid, stupid Maisy!

Orion, Logan, and Kai can hear me for sure, but they're nowhere to be seen. The cold truth sinks in; I'm completely alone, left to endure this harrowing reality by myself. There is no one to turn to, no one to guide me through the relentless darkness that now defines my existence.

ORION

Kai parked his bike and joined us in the car, utterly unaware of what transpired in the last ten minutes. We quickly got him up to speed.

Emilio is fidgeting in the driver's seat while the three of us sit in the back, hypnotized. These are the moments when the blackout windows of my car serve a purpose; we have a clear view of everyone, every face. And through Maisy's mike, we also hear every word people are saying. And still we cannot believe this has happened.

Did we not see it? We did. But I thought it would be her sister, not Christopher.

"Fucking bitch," Logan says under his breath, and I turn to follow his eyeline.

Directly opposite the back exit of the restaurant is a blacked-out limo, and just as the back window is winding up, we see her. Eyeballing Maisy directly, and laughing cruelly. She knew we'd never let her have Maisy, no matter what, so she delivered her straight to the cops.

Just like that, the window closes, and the car takes off.

Amid all the chaos of the cops and other people talking in the background, all that's repeating in my head is Maisy's quiet plea for salvation. *Save me.* Like a dagger stabbed straight in the heart, those words tear me apart.

They said '*the murder of Natasha Wilson.*' I'm not worried about the video, with it being grainy, it won't hold in court, but if Rosey really has the gun, Maisy's fucked. *We're* fucked.

As her lawyer, I will defend her with my life. I've done that already, many times; that's not in question. What I'm most worried about is them getting to her and offering her a new life, away from here, from us, under witness protection. The same way we hoped to clear the Slavs from New York. And she may choose to take up that new life. I know she'll consider it because it would give her everything she's always desired for herself and her sister. Now that Rosey's out of the picture, I know Maisy will have to think of herself. That's why her *Save me* just killed me. It felt like that was the moment when she decided what to do about us.

She knows too much, way too much, and we never planned for her to ever be in this position. Can we trust her? The one question we never truly got an answer to.

"Fuck, she knows too much about everything!" My thoughts are spoken out loud before I realize I'm talking. I glance over at Kai. His fists are clenched with the promise of vengeance. Rosey and Christopher will pay for this.

Logan promptly reminds me of my duty as a lawyer. "Go get her."

I need no reminding when it comes to Maisy. "They're fucking idiots if they think it's gonna be this easy," I growl. "This is the woman of not one, but three mafia heads, and no one's gonna fuck with her."

We all watch as Maisy's fragile form enters the backseat of the police vehicle, her head being gently pushed down as she goes. She looks defeated, her shoulders slumped and her eyes dropped low. There's a blend of resignation and despair on her face.

I leave the car and stride over, reaching them just as most of the cops get in their cars. Christopher left already. Some of them eye me as I get near. I bet they recognize me. They should.

I keep my eyes locked on the car holding Maisy. Its engine revs, ready to pull away. I sprint and reach the vehicle just as it's about to drive off. I tap sharply on the window, my urgency clear.

The cop inside looks over. After sizing me up through the glass, he finally lets the window down. "Yeah?"

I go into full lawyer mode. "May I ask on what grounds you are detaining my client? Probable cause for arrest must be based on concrete evidence, not mere suspicion or circumstantial evidence."

"Your client? And you are?"

"I'm Orion Carte." I nod at Maisy sitting in the back. She hasn't noticed me yet. "Her lawyer."

The officer hesitates, uncertainty etched across his face. He briefly turns his head to seek some hint or direction from his partner, perhaps hoping for guidance on how to handle me.

However, I can tell from his partner's fleeting glance that there's a flicker of recognition there – he knows who I am. Wisely, he offers no help, merely shrugging nonchalantly.

The cop turns back to me. His face broadcasts the internal conflict he's experiencing; his eyes narrow slightly as he mulls over his options. There's a brief moment where the world seems to pause, highlighting the severity of what his next words or actions could mean for him.

I address him again. "If you believe you have enough evidence to take my client into custody, I require a detailed explanation of this evidence and how it links my client to the crime."

"Um, look," he sputters, "we're taking her to the station, so you can take it up with my boss there."

"Wrong. You're gonna release her, to me." I hand him my business card. "You get your boss to contact me whenever he wants."

He doesn't know or understand how things work in New York. His youthful appearance only reinforces my suspicion that his assignment to this particular task was no accident. I can almost see the cogs turning, the way he hesitates and looks around, a clear sign he's grappling with the nuances of the job. It strikes me that they likely chose him for this very reason – because he's unfamiliar with the mafia. So far. This lack of awareness makes him the perfect pawn.

"I don't have all day," I say impatiently.

The cop shrugs and gets out. Before helping Maisy out, he looks around again. Everyone else has left by now. No doubt, they all recognized me and didn't want to deal with the mafia. Good choice.

Maisy has seen me and is crying now; she jumps into my arms before her handcuffs are even off. The cop pulls at her arms and uncuffs her.

I nod at him. "Thank you, officer...?"

"Zack. Zack Videnov."

"Thank you, Zack. When your boss calls me, I'll make sure to put in a good word for you." Maisy's weeping inconsolably in my embrace. "Shhh, it's okay. I got you."

I wrap my arm around her waist and raise my free hand to signal Emilio to pick us up.

CHAPTER 14

MAISY

"Why, why would they say that?" I bawl, wrapped in Kai's arms on our way to Logan's tower.

Christopher orchestrated this whole thing to have me arrested. Or was it Rosie? How could I have been so blindly stupid? So stupid to meet him? So stupid to kill Natasha? In front of everyone, too!

"Please stop crying, we'll figure something out," Kai says in an attempt to soothe me, but all of a sudden, that same influx of nausea comes forth.

"Stop the car, I'm gonna throw up!" I yell.

"Keep driving, Emilio," Orion orders, so I lean down to retch between Kai's legs. My stomach lurches a few times but nothing comes up. It's unpleasant, and quite painful as my abdomen contracts.

"It's the adrenaline," Orion insists. "She'll be fine."

Feeling lousy, I wipe the drool from my chin. "He said that he saw a video of me shooting Natasha, and that Rosey has the gun. Why didn't you pick it up after I killed her? And how do they know? No one was there, apart from your men!"

"There must've been video surveillance of the whole place." Orion strokes my back. "Don't worry Maisy, we'll find a way out of this."

I turn to him, my throat tight from crying. "Out of this?? The police wanted to take me away!" I yell in his face. "They nearly succeeded, you know! What took you so long?"

Orion doesn't say a word. I'm right. He took ages to show up.

"Tell me, what happened?" I cry.

"Sweetheart..." Logan gently turns my chin toward him. "We said this would be a trap and it was. Please, I beg you, start listening to us for a change. We know you're smart, but we've been in this business since birth, and trying to navigate through it on your own often leaves you either dead or in jail. Rosey just found a way to put you behind bars. *That's* what happened."

My desperation turns to anger. "Fucking Slavs! I've had it with them!" I wipe away my tears and move to sit next to Kai. I don't need anyone hugging me anymore.

I'm not the meek, helpless Maisy Roy. I'm Maisy fucking Slavinovich, and fuck me if don't have in me some of that nasty blood. I have it, and I will use it. Against all of them.

"We must get hold of that video," I say. "And the gun."

Kai and Logan look at me, then each other, probably surprised by my rage.

Orion locks eyes with me and nods. "Chrstopher said the video is grainy, so I'm not worried about that. What we need to do is get hold of the gun."

"We go first thing tomorrow." My voice is still shaky, but my determination is solid.

"Maisy, it's never a good idea when you come with," Orion argues. "Haven't you learned that by now?"

"I don't care. I'm not hiding anymore. I'm not gonna wait for you to save me. I've had it. I'm coming. And I'm gonna end this once and for all. There aren't that many Slavs left, and your people can handle it."

Logan raises his eyebrows. "Now you wanna involve our families?"

"You were gonna have a war sooner or later. It's better sooner. Oh, *fuck*." I retch some more, nauseous once again. "I think I'm hungry."

Kai's concerned. "When was the last time you ate, Maisy?"

"Must've been last night."

"Goddamn, Maisy! You gotta eat breakfast!" Logan snaps.

"Actually, this could make sense." Orion's the only one considering my plan. "They wouldn't expect us tomorrow. They think Maisy's in custody. If we attack in the morning, we'll have the element of surprise. They'll be unprepared."

"The Delgados are ready whenever I tell them," Kai announces.

Logan nods. "The Vitalis, too."

"Then tomorrow it is." Orion nods as the car stops outside Vitali Tower. "You feeling better?" he asks me.

I shrug. "I dunno. I feel like a train hit me. I'm tired, everything hurts, my heart's hammering in my chest, and I can't shake this feeling of doom."

~

The intel they got made them move up their attack to tonight instead of tomorrow. I'm going with them, but deep down, who are we kidding? I know they'll keep me protected. And I'll end up on the sidelines again. Until I have enough of being shielded, and decide to go out all guns blazing. And most likely end up dead. Or, at least, one of us will. I hate that it reminds me of everything that happened at the Gianini restaurant.

So, of course, I have my own plan. One that won't get them too annoyed, because they'd be going to the Slav HQ anyway. What it would do is give me time to get to Rosey and ask her why. Why did she have to go down that route? Have me arrested? If Orion hadn't taken me from the police car, my life would've been over. Still, if we don't find that gun, my life *will* definitely be over. I'll end up in jail. And that, I can't do. She kicked me and punched me when I was her prisoner, but she would never kill me. I know that. She's my sister. So I'm going there to ask her why.

Logan said this is my home, that I'll be living with them from now on, and that I should get used to the world they're in. What none of them acknowledge is that I do know their world, and I've been imprisoned in it for far too long.

Kai's talking to his family about joining us tonight. Everyone's eager to get this done. They've lost too much money, and too many people. "The sooner we hit them, the better," is the consensus.

I counted the Slav families relocated by Christopher, and realized there are not that many Slavs left in HQ. Which gives me hope that I'll be able to get inside undetected. My aim is to talk to Rosey, and get the gun. I know the moment they're there, the Cartes, Delgados, and Vitalis will want everyone dead.

But even after everything she's done to me, I don't want Rosey dead. And somehow, I'm afraid that that's the only outcome of tonight. That's why it's imperative that I warn her. To tell her to leave. I don't want my only family member to die. No matter what she's done.

The details are still being discussed in the living room; we're due to leave in one hour, so I excuse myself and head to the roof deck, "to practice my aim," I mutter. They gave me a gun earlier and I've been playing with it, trying to see if I remember how to use it, load it, and so on.

None of them bat an eyelid at me.

The moment I reach the deck, I write a quick note.

"I'm giving myself a head start. I must talk to Rosey. One final conversation. See you there. Love, Maisy."

I remove my clothes and leave the balaclava they gave me on the chair, change into jeans and a t-shirt, grab my tote bag with a towel and some body oil inside, one of mine, and put a COVID mask on my face. There were a few lying around the penthouse, which gave me the idea to enter Rosey's house as a masseuse. I text for an Uber, then leave my cell on the roof deck. I quickly head to the fire escape and begin descending. It will take me a few minutes to get to street level, but at least no one will be there. I know everyone's being mobilized and no one will be standing guard on the street.

Just as I drop down to street level, my Uber pulls up. I look nonchalantly left and right, making sure no one sees me. There's a camera up on the wall, but that's fine. They'll soon know where I am, and it's not that I don't want them to follow. I just want a head start.

"Uber for Maisy?"

"Yes. Heading to Greenwich Avenue, Central Valley?"

The driver nods. I enter and he pulls away as quickly as he came.

The drive takes an hour and all the while, I try to keep my mind free of the self-defeating thoughts that attack me from every angle. No, I won't die. No, she won't kill me. Yes, I'm safe. I keep the internal chatter under control and start thinking about what exactly I'll tell Rosey. After she kidnapped me, imprisoned me, beat me, prepared me for rape – thank God that didn't happen – after all that, what can I say to her that would get me heard? I get why Orion wants her dead. And Logan. And Kai, too.

But not me.

Am I a glutton for punishment? I probably am. But she's my little sister. She'll always be my little sister.

The driver rouses me from my internal monologue. "We're here."

I look up and yes, there it is. This is the place I said I would never go back to. And this is the place I keep going back to. By force, or otherwise.

I check the front entrance. There's only one person standing on guard.

"Thank you. Have a good night."

I gather all my strength and, as if I'm not walking straight to my death, I exit the car and make my way to the front door.

The guard stands up straight upon seeing me. He's trying to figure me out. I'm wearing a face mask, so I doubt he'll recognize me.

He gives me a toothless scowl. "Yeah?"

"I'm here to see Rosey. She called in a masseuse, and they told me to come here."

Eyeing me carefully, he orders, "Remove your mask."

I pull it up from my chin to my nose, the perfect way to not show my full face. "I'm sorry, I'm vulnerable without it. Poor immune system and stuff."

He snorts dismissively. "Lemme see what's in your bag."

I open the bag and show him the sole two items. I don't even have my cell with me to go back to Logan's. I'm counting on the boys to pick me up. Dead or alive. Either, at this point. This is the last thing I'll do on my own. But I have to. She has the gun I killed Natasha with.

Why I threw it on the lawn that night, I have no idea. Well, actually, I do. I thought there was honor among thieves. Or at least sisters. I'm not that lucky, I guess. Here I am, trying to warn her to leave, while she sold me out to the authorities. Ugh. Thinking about how stupid I am is driving me crazy. It's like I'm trying to make myself stupider on purpose; that's why I keep giving her another chance, like saying *'Look at me, Rosey, I'm stupid, and I can be your friend.'*

"Alright. Go in." The man opens the door for me. "Been here before?"

"Yes."

He dismisses me, and shuts the door once I'm inside.

My heart hammers in my chest as I realize I'm standing on my own in the huge entrance. There's not a living soul in sight. I take a step forward into the house and try to remember: if I keep to the left, and then go down the corridor, at the end should be the door I'm after, the door to Milan's office. Which is now Rosey's.

I start walking and soon see the office, and spot two men chatting outside it. The one with bushy eyebrows and scars on his face, I recognize from the first time I paid her a visit.

I'm dreading passing them, but I know that's the only place Rosey will be. As I approach, I realize how very afraid I am. The adrenaline rushing through my veins is unsettling. I'm inside the Slav headquarters on my own, heading past the two guards, straight for Rosey's office. I pray she's in there.

"Who are you?" The one with scars on his face demands and I freeze. I mustn't show fear. That's all I'm thinking about.

"I'm Rosey's masseuse. And who are you?" I respond, despite my voice trembling.

"I'm Rob." He says with a smirk. "She should be in her office."

"Um, okay. Rob."

I turn around and take a few more steps before I stop outside the door to collect myself. Once I've taken a few breaths to calm my nerves, I raise my hand to knock. That's when her voice scares me to death.

"Who the fuck are you?" she screeches from behind me.

I turn around and gape at her; she gapes right back at me. And she's furious. Up close, she looks like she hasn't slept for days. Her top is stained and threadbare. Last time I was here, she looked all pristine and in control. I can't imagine what's happened in between. Maybe we got to her?

"That's your masseuse, boss." Rob proudly informs her.

"My masseuse? Can't you tell, you idiots? That's my sister! And you two just let her waltz in here. She could've killed me!" She pulls her gun and aims at them. "You're lucky I need people right now. Make one more mistake and you're dead!"

"I'm sorry, Rosey," the other one mutters.

Rob just lowers his head. "Won't happen again, boss."

"Don't apologize to me – go outside, see who she came with, idiots!"

She hits Rob on the head, then sends them away. Then, she aims her gun at me and comes closer. Each step she takes makes that muzzle closer and bigger. I'm so scared I can barely move.

She presses the tip firmly against my forehead, making me take an instinctive step back. The back of my head hits the door of her office.

"Inside, now!" she orders.

I'm staring at her, terrified, as my hand scrambles blindly behind me for the handle of the door. Upon finding it, I press down; the door swings open and I tumble to the floor.

"Get up!" She points the gun across the room. I stagger to my feet and follow where she's gesturing. "Over there. Sit."

I turn around in search of a chair, and quickly find the one I sat in the last time I was here. The large desk is here too, but there aren't boxes everywhere anymore. No paperwork either. The office has been completely cleared. All of Milan's boxes that stood for years in this office are gone.

After closing the door, Rosey sits down behind the desk and leans back in her chair.

She despises me, and I think she's close to killing me, but I don't hold it against her. I would never let her get hurt. I know what happened to her. This is not the Rosey I knew. Milan brainwashed her. If I had saved her in time, we would be fighting on the same side now. It's all my fault. And if I can make it right, I will. Even if it costs me my life.

"Why do you keep coming back?" Rosey sounds resigned, her shoulders slump, and her voice is... softer?

I clear my throat. "For you. For *you*, Rosey. You're my sister, no matter what you've done to me, or what you're gonna do to me."

She shakes her head, dismissive.

"*And* for your children," I add. "Maxim, Luca, Damien, and Mila."

She raises her eyebrows at me. *Yes, I remember their names.*

"Why are you surprised? I have no one in this world who's family, and you had only me before you had children. I want to be part of your family. I want your kids to know who I am."

"I don't see the point in thinking about the future," she says indifferently. "Things are gonna fall apart, like they always do."

"Rosey, please, there *is* a way out," I urge. "I can connect you with Christopher and he can put you in witness protection, with your children. You can have a new life, far away from here."

"Oh, fuck *off!*" she shouts abruptly, as if she thinks I'm mocking her. "Shut the fuck up. Who do you think you are, Mother Teresa? I don't need anyone. No one! You hear me?! Milan's dead, and I'm free. Do you even have any idea what that means? Have you ever been free in your life? Well, I have. I *am*. And it's fucking amazing. I make my own destiny!" She suddenly fires a shot at the ceiling, making me duck. I cover my head as the ear-splitting sound is followed by dust and debris falling from the damaged tile.

"After all the sacrifices I made, I get no thanks, Maisy. So why bother? Why run, when you could stay and kill as many fuckers as you can?"

She aims her gun at me.

"Don't shoot, Rosey. It would break Mom's heart." I'm still shaking inside from that gunshot, but I have to try a different approach. *One last try.* "If she could see you now, she wouldn't approve of what you're doing."

"And she would of you?" she sneers. "You shot someone point-blank, Maisy! Point-blank, in the face! Like an assassin! I saw the video."

"Yeah, but she would've–"

"She would've what?! She was a human being, too!" Rosey's humanity is just about eking through the façade she's putting up. That, there, is my real sister who I love and cherish. And for that, I will not let any harm come to her.

"Rosey, you don't understand..."

"*I* don't understand?" She yells. "You know, I've had it with you, and everyone else here. I'm sending you straight to prison. That's where you belong. To live the kind of life I lived while you were free. Up! On your feet! I'm taking you to the police myself!"

"Rosey, no, I didn't mean–"

"Shut up!"

I rise to my feet and turn around with my hands raised in surrender, instantly feeling the pressure of the muzzle at my back as she follows closely behind. I reach for the door, pulling it open, and together we step out into the corridor.

"Who did she come with? Did you find out?" she asks Rob and his goon who have resumed standing guard outside the office.

"We didn't see anyone. She arrived in a cab, and the car left already," The goon replies.

"Right. Keep your eyes and ears open, dumbass," she says. "Rob, zip tie her hands behind her back."

Without missing a beat, Rob retrieves a zip tie from his pocket and swiftly spins me around. He grabs both of my hands and attempts to secure them. Just before he pulls them tight, a burst of machine-gun fire erupts from outside. *They're here!*

Rosey's eyebrows draw together tightly and her face morphs into fierce anger, eyes narrowing into thin slits. "You!"

I pull my wrists free and reach for the gun she's holding; my fingers wrap possessively around the handle and try to snatch it. She has a firm hold on it; we start to wrestle and fall to the ground.

"Rosey, there's still time, I can save you! Please, listen to me!" I plead. I'm trying to take sole control of the gun, we both are, but I'm trying to save her too.

"What are you waiting for?! Kill her! *KILL HER!*" she shrieks as she fights with all her strength to overpower me.

"Um, boss, I can't. You're both moving, I could kill you."

All of a sudden, the gun discharges between us, startling us both. Despite the shock, I refuse to let go. So does Rosey. There's a thud behind me. I dare not look back, but I can hear Rob swearing.

"You killed someone *else*, you bitch!" Rosey yells. "Let go of the gun!"

"You're the one holding the gun! You killed him! Give it to me!"

CHAPTER 15

ORION

We're descending in the elevator, and I'm boiling with anger. Everybody around me is equally furious. We're ready to attack the Slavs, our final fight, to kill each and every one that remains, and my face is burning with rage. I swear I'm gonna lock that woman up in a room, never to see the sun again.

"Why the fuck did we trust her, someone tell me?!" I growl.

"We didn't know she was gonna do this," Kai protests, as if to absolve us of our stupidity.

"Really? Really, Kai? We didn't?" I tilt my head at him, waiting for an excuse.

"Okay, we should've suspected." He raises his hands in defeat. "But we thought she'd put all that behind her."

"Maisy's one helluva stubborn woman. But she's *our* woman," Logan sighs.

"I'm not sure I want her like this," I mutter under my breath.

The elevator door opens and the first thing we see is the clock on the wall, showing it's exactly ten. Everyone has congregated in the reception hall. Our plan is clear: penetrate the Slav headquarters, kill as many people as possible. That's it. That's all they need to know, anyway. Of course, there is another plan for us – one where we find the gun Maisy killed Natash with. And now, we have to find Maisy too, and make sure they don't kill her.

"God, she annoys the hell out of me!" I hiss under my breath.

The Cartes and Delgados have already arrived, and are parked outside waiting for us.

"Are you all ready?" Logan asks Uncle Jon.

Uncle Jon looks at his men standing behind him. "Ready as we'll ever be."

We all leave the tower at the same time. The Vitalis go to their cars, the Delgados and Cartes are revving up their engines, and Emilio's car's running, ready. He too wears a balaclava.

"She has a fifteen to twenty-minute head start," I say once the three of us are in the car.

"Should we drive faster?" Logan asks.

"We stick to the plan," I say.

"Let's hope we're on time," Kai mutters, staring out of the window.

About forty-five minutes later, I spot the house. The plan is to park out of their line of sight and stealthily approach, catching them off-guard. The Cartes will enter from the north, the Delgados from the southwest, and as for us, we're entering from the east, the far end of the backyard, together with the Vitalis.

Fucking Maisy. I can't believe I have to keep saying *fucking Maisy.* Why does she always have to go against our orders?

We leave the car and as planned, make our way through the backyards. Armed with my trusted Colt and a flashlight, I'm plowing through each property with everyone else following me when I notice a square mottled-stone memorial hiding in the grass.

"Careful not to trip." I aim my flashlight at the stonework and nod to everyone behind me.

We make it through and now, up close to the house, we hide behind the bushes. I lead, with Kai and Logan next to me and a team of five men following us.

"Spread out," I whisper, and point with my gun to the area I want them to cover.

As an unwritten rule, we are to use our guns as a last resort. We don't want to warn the Slavs too early that we're here.

From where I'm standing, I can see three men in front of us, standing watch. I tuck my Colt back into its holster as I wait for the right moment to attack. When the man closest to me turns his back, I jump out from behind the bushes and hook my arm around his neck, intending to suffocate him quietly. But he's stronger than I anticipated, and manages to slide out of my grip and hit me in the stomach. Ha, he doesn't know that's my game, so I give him three lefts and a right to the face. It's been a while since I sparred with anyone. He stumbles back with blood gushing from his nose.

Before the other two guards catch on to what's happening, Kai swings into action and punches the backs of their heads, one then the other. But he drops and curls up like a shrimp, and I realize that a fourth person behind him is raining punches on him. Logan whips his blades quickly and a thud is heard soon after.

The two remaining men reach for their dropped guns, but before either can pull the trigger, one of our men manages to kick them away from their hands. Finally, Logan hurls more blades at them, fatally wounding both.

"About fucking time," I hiss, and point to the house. "Proceed."

Out of the blue, we hear machine-gun fire coming from the southwest, where the Delgados entered. *Of course.* All of them have short fuses and quick fingers.

I guess it's started. "Shit! Eyes up, everyone! Maisy's our top priority!" I pull out my Colt again.

Logan snorts. "I thought she pissed you off."

"She does. And right now, you're pissing me off too, asshole!"

Kai and Logan chuckle behind me, but stop when we hear shots fired from the north, where the Cartes are.

"Come on, let's get inside!"

There's a man lying on the ground outside the back entrance; we step over him and enter the building.

"We're first in, be careful!" I warn.

The three of us enter silently amid the sound of more gunshots being fired behind the house. There's some kind of commotion inside, too, and we run toward the noise.

"For fuck's sake, *KILL HER!*" I hear Rosey yelling, and then I see them on the ground. She and Maisy are brawling over possession of a gun. Beside them lies a dead man, and another with a scar on his face stands with a gun aimed at them.

The moment he lays eyes on us, he panics and aims at us, although it's clear he's outnumbered. The three of us have our guns trained on him.

Rosey and Maisy are still wrestling on the floor. They grapple ferociously, each maneuver clumsier than the last, reminding me of sisters squabbling over something trivial. Maisy's face is red and her eyes are watering from the strain. Just when Rosey seems on the brink of defeat, she reverses their positions.

With a huge effort, Maisy manages to wrench the gun from Rosey's hand and throw it aside. It slides along the floor and stops directly in front of the scar face. He swiftly drops to one knee, snatching up the gun. Now he's holding two.

Maisy and Rosey disentangle, their chests heaving.

"Thank fuck!" Rosey points at us. "Rob, kill them, let's get this over and done with!"

"I wouldn't do that if I was you," I warn him. He's a dead man. He knows that. We know that. What we don't know is if he's stupid enough to fire his gun.

Tall, lanky, in scruffy-looking jeans and a red shirt, he has one gun pointing unwaveringly at Maisy and Rosey, and the other aimed at us.

"What are you waiting for? Are you stupid or something?" Rosey snaps. She clearly doesn't understand what it means to have a gun pointed at her. Or she's had it happen too many times and she's numb to it.

I'm gripping my gun, my finger twitching on the trigger, and my eyes lock with the scarface's. The standoff feels like a chess match with human pawns, where every slight movement is a precursor to checkmate.

Then, in a split second, I see it: the dark resolve in his eyes. He's made his decision. He's going for Maisy, and the hell am I gonna let him get away with that.

His finger squeezes the trigger and a single shot rings out, echoing off the walls.

Immediately, as if rehearsed, we react in a unified surge of fury and vengeance. Before we can see who got shot, we empty our rounds into his body. He topples backward, both guns slipping from his grasp as the life bleeds out of him.

My eyes shoot to Maisy and relief washes over me. The scarface made the right decision. Maisy's alive, and the scream filling the air is hers as she falls to her knees beside Rosey, who's collapsed to the floor, blood pouring out of her mouth.

If I didn't know any better, I'd say the scene before my eyes was tragic. Maisy cradles Rosey's head in her lap, her hands trembling as she attempts to staunch the flow of blood spreading across her sister's chest.

MAISY

"No! No! Rosey, wake up!" I can do nothing to stop the blood oozing from the gunshot wound. "Someone do something!"

Rosey manages to crack a half-smile. "Maisy…"

"I'm so sorry, Rosey, I'm so sorry I didn't save you. I'm sorry…" I whisper through my tears, my voice choked with a grief I didn't know I could ever possibly feel. "Please don't leave me."

Rosey's hand reaches up, a weak gesture, to touch my cheek. "It's not… your fault," she manages, her words a labored whisper.

Her hand falls away, her strength ebbing as I pull her closer, my sobs growing louder, more desperate. "Don't leave me here alone," I plead. The heartbreak is crushing me, tearing me in half. I clutch onto my sister, my twin. I never want to let her go. She is part of my life, we shared a womb; we shared *everything* until Milan came into our lives and tore us apart. And even then I searched for her. I did everything to find her, but it was too late.

Rosey's breaths grow shallower. "Take care of… my children."

"I will, I promise." The sound of my weeping fills the air as I lie down next to my sister.

"They'll want to meet your baby," she gasps, barely audibly.

"M-My baby?"

Rosey gives me one last heart-wrenching, knowing smile, and the light completely fades from her eyes, leaving behind a silence too profound to bear and a reality too difficult to comprehend.

"No! No, Rosey! Rosey!" I cling to her and shake her, but someone's arms are pulling me from her. Whoever it is, they're stronger than me, and I sob as I'm forcefully taken away.

"Maisy, come on, you gotta go before the cops get here." It's Orion holding me. "Emilio will drive you home while we search for the gun."

"Logan?" comes Kai's hushed voice.

"Maybe she's been sick for a different reason," Logan replies equally quietly as he strokes my back.

CHAPTER 16

ORION

"Good afternoon, everyone! We called you here today for a few reasons. One, you may already know." I pause and glance at Logan and Kai, who are sitting on either side of me. A full glass of whiskey rests in front of each of us. Kai's face shows conviction and thoughtfulness. Logan's mouth is set in a firm, straight line.

The three of us exude authority. Logan is in a beige three-piece suit, as am I, except mine is my trademark black, and Kai is in his element in his leather gear. Nothing has changed. We are who we are. Except, our front from now on will be a united one.

We're at the Delgados' bar, a place we chose because it's free of wiretaps and there's no surveillance within, except theirs, of course. Basically, it's clean from any eavesdropping. Plus, it's actually big enough for all of our families to gather. There's still pressure from the police about the Slav massacre, but to the world, this is a bar and we're drinking. And right now, the whole bar is silent, waiting on me to speak.

And speak, I do. "The Slav syndicate has been destroyed!"

A big cheer erupts. My uncles, Logan's uncle, and everyone else throw their hands up in the air; many applaud, and the whole place is vibrant with energy. A few champagne corks pop in the air.

I stand up and raise my glass. Logan and Kai follow.

"To us! The Cartes! The Vitalis! The Delgados!"

Everyone else raises their glasses too, and we all drain them in unison in a smooth, swift motion. The moment the last drops are gulped down, we simultaneously slam our glasses back onto the table, creating a clatter that echoes the crowd's excitement.

"Salut!"

Everyone drinks again. And everyone rejoices.

I fill our glasses with yet more whiskey, lift the glass in my hand again, as do Logan and Kai, and raise my free hand for the crowd to quiet down.

"And to our fallen men!"

I intentionally spill some of my drink on the floor and down the remainder, the strong liquid burning a trail down my throat. Around me, others follow suit, each person's small spill marking a symbolic tribute, a liquid offering for those we've lost. The room is filled with a somber unity, the act of spilling our drinks serving as a collective remembrance of the sacrifices made.

My thoughts drift to Garry. He was just a kid, really, far too young to have been caught in our crossfire.

"*Salut!*" echoes around the room.

I clear my throat. "The Slavs did a lot of racketeering, illegal waste dumping, money laundering, and drug trafficking. And other fucked-up stuff we don't wanna know about! They also had a lot of help from extremely powerful people in New York and beyond. Who are they? We don't know, but I wanna show them that there's a new boss in town."

There is a brief silence as everyone considers my words, which I made deliberately vague.

Soon, a murmuring swell follows as people begin to whisper among themselves, asking each other if anyone understood what I meant.

The question is finally called out. "Who's the new boss?"

Some of them are unsure how to react and instinctively reach for their guns. The atmosphere has shifted to something more unsettled.

"To answer that question, I have to tell you the other reason why we're here today."

Immediate silence falls, quiet enough for me to hear my ever-running thoughts.

It's been two weeks since we left the Slav HQ burning to ashes. Rosey's body was in there, together with the other dead bodies that were brought in just before we lit it up. To get rid of the evidence. After the whole thing was over, and the police identified the bodies, her body was the only one we claimed. Maisy wanted to give her a proper burial. "She deserves so much more," she said. It kills me to see her hurting. But grieving is a process. It cannot be rushed.

Although, if there was a way to change that, I'd find it. All she does lately is cry. We don't know what to do. She doesn't want to talk to anyone, staying cooped up in her room at Logan's. She'll be out when she feels better, she said.

It's been two long fucking weeks that she hasn't come out.

One thing we're happy about is that she's eating, at least. None of us is saying it but I think there's a possibility that she could, in fact, be pregnant. We agreed that if she is, we'll get it dealt with. We haven't played with her as long as we want yet. So, no babies.

Babies.

That word is... unthinkable. But could she have become pregnant that easy? I hear all the time about women having trouble getting pregnant; it takes months, if not years. The mere thought of bringing a child, my child, into this world incapacitates me. Knowing that they'd have to go through everything I did. Living in the mafia world demands a lot of courage. It's a life filled with constant danger and uncertainty. The environment is ruthless, the trust is scarce, and loyalty is often tested.

A definite no.

Because it would mean that one of us, or one of my brothers, made a baby with a Slav. Surely that bloodline should be killed off.

Fuck. What am I even thinking?

This brings to mind how I found Rosey's children. I know Maisy will want to adopt them. But, again, what would that look like?

In our ruthless world, a place where many of our friends were killed by the Slavs, we would be raising four of them? Fuck that. It's not gonna happen.

Yesterday, I got two letters addressed to Maisy. As Maisy's lawyer, I'm dealing with the legalities on her behalf. She claimed her sister's body already, and now, according to the letter from child services, they want her to sign a consent form so they can find those kids a home. The second letter was from the estate's will. After Rosey, the house, or what was left of it, belongs to Maisy.

Fuck. I have this void in my life, and it's because of her. I miss her. We all do.

"Tell us, already!" someone shouts from the crowd, and I'm brought back to the Delgados' bar with all these people standing in front of me.

Logan places his hand on my shoulder. "You got this!"

"Good luck, because I wouldn't know where to start," Kai mutters.

"Right." I look around at everyone. "It all started when Maisy Roy, or as you now know, Maisy Slavinovich, showed up at my house."

"Let's hope she's not the new boss!" someone shouts, and the whole crowd bursts into laughter.

Logan and Kai snicker, but I'm sure they realize that Maisy runs our lives and we run the lives of everyone else here. Like second-hand smoke, she is affecting them. I laugh inwardly.

I raise my hand, signaling to everyone to quiet down. "We've been uncovering things for months, ever since the war with the Slavs started last year. What we discovered was, in short, this." I look at Logan, then at Kai, and smile. "The three of us are half-brothers."

Silence descends again, before a shriek of laughter fills the room. More people cackle and join in. Apparently, this is a joke.

I don't understand what's so funny. I glance over at Logan, who's frowning, and then at Kai, whose jaw tightens at the audacity of someone laughing at him. I suppose we have to understand that the concept of us being a family was a no-go until only a short while ago.

Explaining this is going to be difficult. Amid the noise, I spot Tom, the older man in the weathered leather jacket that looks like it hasn't been taken off since the last time we saw him here, making his way toward us. He walks up and stops in front of the crowd, then turns to face them all.

"It's true," he announces, and turns to Kai. "Your father told me. I had to keep it confidential. It's how it was." He shrugs.

"Who's this old man?" one of the Cartes shouts out.

A couple of Vitalis jeer. "He's drunk, take him away!"

But as the crowd notices the stunned expressions on the Delgados' faces, the mood quickly changes.

Kai looks floored. "You knew?"

Tom nods.

Everyone looks to be in shock. Before I let myself get distracted, I focus on finishing my speech.

"And so, when I say one boss, I mean one syndicate. We're not gonna have three separate families fighting on the streets of New York."

"Is this right, Logan?" Uncle Jon interjects. He seems in a hurry to stop Logan from saying something he could regret. "I know your father hated Willer and Mickey."

"Uncle Jon, we checked twice," Logan tells him, and then addresses the crowd. "Everyone, who remembers, around thirteen years ago, when my father took me to the deserted factory over in Brooklyn and pitted me against Kai and Orion? He told me I was to make my first kill that day."

"I remember that," Uncle Jon says.

"Yeah, me too," Uncle Colletti says. "I was there."

Tom nods, along with a few other men in the crowd.

"That was the day Kai, Orion, and I met. And it was the day we made a pact, to watch each other's backs."

Logan steps in between Kai and me, placing his hands on our shoulders. "We didn't really need a DNA test to tell us we're brothers. We knew that a long time before we actually found out."

"So... you... you talked to each other all this time?" Zeena asks.

"Yeah," Kai confirms.

"How is it possible?" someone shouts.

"That's a different conversation. I'm sure you'll find out soon," I say.

"I think this calls for a celebration!" Uncle Leo exclaims. "All drinks are on me!"

The crowd goes wild at the notion of free drinks.

LOGAN

In the last year, I fell in love with Maisy, I nearly died for her a few times, tried killing her, and almost died again.

The life I've lived matches one from a movie. A life on the edge. Especially the last part, just before we burned the Slav headquarters down.

While Orion got Maisy out of the house, Kai and I started ransacking it, searching for the gun. We had to find it before the police came, and time was not on our side. The shooting was heard far and wide and they were already on their way. It was lucky for us that the local cops did not want to deal with the New York mafia and were waiting for backup from the city.

We knew the Slavs had a way of recruiting people, and therefore there must have been a stash somewhere of all the videos people were being blackmailed with. And searching for it felt like a long process. We were tearing walls down, breaking furniture; basically, we were destroying anything in our path.

One thing we asked our men was for any dead bodies to be brought inside the house. We knew we'd torch the house when we were done. There was no chance we were leaving evidence for the cops; that was always the plan.

With Orion back, we decided to stay longer and thoroughly search every corner before leaving.

And just when we were running out of time, under the large desk in the office I spotted a small latch in the floor. I pulled on it and there it was: the jackpot. We uncovered a small bunker equipped with advanced technology, wiretaps, hidden microphones, and other forms of electronic monitoring. Milan, and in the last few months, Rosey, must have intercepted hundreds of communications regarding illegal activities, plans for future crimes, or the identities of individuals for whatever reasons they needed them. All the tapes were neatly stacked on one side. And on a shelf, just above the main desk, was a gun with a tape next to it. Kai recognized it as his own gun, the one Maisy shot Natasha with.

"We got what we needed! Burn the house down!" Orion ordered, and took the gun and tape. We were going to personally make sure those were properly destroyed.

I pulled Orion out of the bunker, and as we were leaving, Kai, who had been starting the fires, torched the room. Soon, the fire was eating up everything it reached.

We left the office and moved through the other rooms, setting each one ablaze in turn. Soon after we got out, the whole house was engulfed in flames.

We retreated the same way we got in, through the backyard, and even though our escape route was lit up by the flames, Kai somehow managed to trip on a square stone, the one we'd tried to avoid earlier. He fell to the ground, having injured his foot. Had he not done that, we wouldn't have seen the name on the memorial stone: R.T.

Right then, as we were wondering if this was where Rebecca Trellis was buried, the whole house collapsed in a pile of ash and rubble. No Slav was left alive.

Except Maisy. She's a Slav. But she's ours.

As for the stone, we knew we would be going back there when the dust settled.

When we told everyone about us being brothers, the reviews were mixed. Some loved it; some, the greedier ones, didn't. They knew with more people in the operation, there'd be less money to split. Tough luck.

But our men are the least of our worries. We set up a meeting between Uncle Jon, Uncle Leo, and Tom.

One representative from each family, to agree the terms. Simple. We needed to remove ourselves from everything and focus on Maisy.

She's been cooped up in her room all this time. And all she does is eat. Which I'm really grateful for, but I want her. My cock aches every night, and when I jerk off, I think of her thighs, of her ass, and of slamming inside her body the way she wants it.

Fuck. I don't know what else to think about.

I need her.

My only consolation is that she's with me, in my penthouse. No one has complained about it and she seems to like it here. She hasn't said anything either, but I know she'll speak up if she doesn't like something. Just like she threw away the pregnancy tests I've been bringing her with each meal.

From a doctor's perspective, it's imperative that we know whether a woman is pregnant so we can provide the needed support.

But from a man's perspective, I'm fucked.

I know we all agreed that if she's pregnant, we'll get it aborted, though it's true that we didn't ask for her opinion. However, am I crazy for thinking that I don't want to go down that route? I would never admit it, because an agreement is an agreement, but fuck. I'm split in half.

One half of me wants to have sex free of consequences with Maisy until we all turn eighty, and the other half wants to procreate with her for the next twenty years.

"Logan?"

I jump, startled. Fuck. I'm in my bed, lying in the dark in my boxer shorts, staring at the lights of Manhattan through the windows. I did not expect her at all. My cock's okay with it, though; my hard-on is jutting up and making a tent in my shorts. "Maisy, are you okay? Is everything good?"

"Can I lie next to you?" she breathes softly. Wearing a skimpy white top and white panties, she looks angelic. Her hair's messy, though; I'm not sure if she's brushed it at all for weeks.

"Come here, sweetheart." I lift the sheet and invite her to lie next to me.

She climbs into the bed and rests her head in the crook of my neck. This is all I've been thinking about for the last three weeks. I cover her with the sheet and wrap my arms around her.

"I missed you," I whisper, smelling her hair.

She makes herself comfortable, draping her arm across my body and her leg across mine, pressing her body close to me. "Me too," she sighs.

CHAPTER 17

KAI

"Hold the door!" I call.

The box I'm carrying prevents me from running. Instead, I walk briskly across the reception hall to the elevator at Logan's tower. I saw someone in a tailored suit entering just before me. I couldn't tell, but I'd bet my life it was Orion. His jacket was in his hand, his vest buttoned up, and the sleeves of his shirt were rolled up to the elbow. "Orion!"

I see the doors closing but at the last moment, a hand adorned with four silver rings emerges to hold them open.

"Oh, hey, Kai," says Orion.

"Didn't you hear me yelling at you?"

"Naah. Was in a world of my own."

"I bet. Logan texted to say Maisy's sleeping with him and you couldn't get here quick enough."

"Ha, so you heard, too?"

"Fuck, yeah. You think he'd text you and not me?"

"I don't think anything. Right now, my cock's doing the thinking."

"Do you think they're up?"

"Don't know. Uncle Jon opened the elevator doors for me. What's in the box?"

"Stuff I wanted to go through a while back." I adjust my groin, making space in my jeans, and wiggle my eyebrows. "Do you think she'll be up for a round of hanky-panky?"

"As long as you call it 'hanky-panky,' she won't be. I assure you."

The doors ping open at the top of the tower, and we hurry into the living room that overlooks the city. I forget what it's like where Logan lives until I'm here, and see all of its majestic view over New York.

Orion doesn't stop and continues down the hallway and, hurriedly, I drop the box on the coffee table and follow him. We're heading straight for Logan's bedroom.

A quick courtesy knock on the door and we're in. No fucking around with Orion. We're met with a brightly lit room; the drapes are pulled open and the early morning sun is beaming through. Logan and Maisy are spooning on the bed, covered with a sheet, just stirring from sleep.

Logan's head is buried in her neck, his leg is draped over her thighs, and his arm's wrapped across her chest. He's holding her tight. I would too if I was in his place. It hurts how much I miss her.

I bet he heard us, but he doesn't bat an eyelid. Maisy's the one who raises her head. She sees us, drops her head back to the pillow, and closes her eyes again, smiling.

"You feeling better, darling?" Orion stands at the foot of the bed, looking her over. And what a view it is. I step forward and join him.

She nods. "Mm-hmm."

Maisy's naked under the sheet, and I notice Logan is too. I don't care about him; he's had her for the night, and it's my turn now.

"Maisy, baby girl, I need you. We all do."

She lifts her head again and looks at me. "I'm here, Kai. I'm here for good."

She pushes back the sheet and stands up on the bed, in front of Orion and me. Being on the bed, she's slightly higher than both of us and I find myself looking up at her as she places a hand on my shoulder.

"Hey, beautiful." I try to sound chill, but all I feel is the kind of adrenaline animals must have when stalking their prey. I could devour her in an instant. *What the fuck is wrong with me?*

My cock is rock-hard right now, but I'm gonna wait until she does something.

"Hey, yourself." Her voice couldn't be sweeter.

Her gentle hands are on my chest, and she peels off my leather jacket first, then scrunches my t-shirt in her fists as she pulls me in. She places her lips to mine, planting on me a kiss I never thought could be so potent. That's it, no going back. My body responds like a lion; I want to eat her alive, that's how much I want her. But I'm gonna let her lead. If it was all up to me, I'd be fucking her already.

She pulls my shirt off and her hands go straight to my jeans, unbuttoning the fly. I glance over at Orion, who's smirking at me, but drinking in her presence as she looks at him, too. Maisy's leg hooks around my hip and she slowly grinds against my cock, moaning quietly in my ear but loud enough for Orion to hear.

That does it. I grab her under her thighs and lift her, pressing my lips to hers, as she moans into my mouth and wraps her legs fully around my waist. Her fingers claw through my long hair and down to my back.

"Kai," she mumbles, sucking on my bottom lip.

"Fuck Maisy, you're driving me crazy," I pant between kisses. Yes, I am acting like a teenager on heat, but fuck me if she's not doing that to me.

I manage to fully shove down my jeans and free up my cock. It juts up out of my boxer shorts, which already have a wet patch from the precum. I grab it and rub it against her entrance. She wants me. If I can tell anything by her level of arousal, I'd say she's been ready for quite some time.

I edge inside her, an inch at a time as she moans. I want to slam inside in one go, but I don't want to cause my baby girl any pain. I groan, because *fuck* it's so hard to go slow. When I'm happy I'm in, I lift her by the butt cheeks and penetrate her again, but this time... fuck, this time I can't help but add some speed.

Her arms wrap around my neck and she pulls my body close to hers, crying out into my mouth at the same time I do. And fuck, am I loud. I begin to pound her, hard and fast, all the while making sure I don't lose my balance. Each thrust into her cunt brings a grunt out of her, which soon becomes staccato as I speed up our rhythm.

"There's my girl," I growl, like an animal. "You like that, don't ya?"

My cock has never been as hard as it is right now. Every time I'm sheathed inside her I'm holding it off for dear life, but it won't last long.

"Kai!" She screams my name as she orgasms, and luckily, I'm there too. I release a deep, guttural groan as I empty my cum into her.

"Fuuuuuckkk!" I'm out of breath, and nearly off-balance, too. I managed to last four whole minutes, I think. Embarrassing, I know, but who cares? The amount of muscle pumping I did in the last three weeks hurt me more.

Maisy grins as I pull out of her. I lay her on the sheet and collapse on it myself, next to Logan.

"Move," I mutter.

Logan laughs as he sits up. "I'm making us coffee. Today, we're celebrating."

"What are we celebrating?" Maisy asks curiously.

"You, sweetheart." He quirks his lips flirtatiously at one corner.

She flushes red and smiles. There's a new shine in her cheeks. Fuck, she's stunning!

Orion has been watching her all this time and still doesn't take his eyes off her. She knows this, and she loves it. She turns and crawls to me on the bed, giving Orion a great view of her raised ass.

"You okay, Kai?" she purrs.

I pull her face to mine and kiss her hard. "With you by my side, I'm better than okay."

Suddenly, there's a smacking sound and Maisy lurches forward slightly, then turns to look back. "Orion?"

"I know you wanted me to do that." He grins darkly. "Now go get dressed. There're lots of updates for you."

"I wanted you–"

"Don't worry, you will," he interrupts teasingly.

She smiles at him wickedly and turns to me. "Come with me, Kai."

I have to kiss her again. This woman has somehow crawled under my skin and is there to stay forever. Like an imprint on my soul.

"Baby girl, I can't. I have something to do. Go get dressed and meet us in the living room."

She frowns playfully and walks out with a stomp, which makes her even cuter.

I stand up and straighten myself out. I pull up my jeans, button up, then take my shirt from the floor and put it on, Orion watching me all the while.

"What?" I ask.

"You. Why didn't you go with Maisy? You've talked about her every hour for the past three weeks."

"I wanted to show you and Logan something. Come," I say, and drag him along toward the living room.

Logan's holding a coffee cup when we walk in. Sitting on the end of the couch, wearing beige slacks and a black polo shirt, reading the newspaper, he looks nothing like the mafia head that he is. He's too sophisticated. I'd say he reminds me of a doctor, getting ready to go to work.

Upon seeing us, he nods at the box I left on the coffee table. "What's with that?"

Orion takes a cup of coffee and sits in the chair facing Logan. He takes a long sip. "Good coffee," he mumbles.

I make myself comfortable on the couch and set the box in my lap. "Something I found at home." I pick up my cup from the table, take a sip, and put it back. "I wanna go through it."

"Why here?" Logan asks, sounding uninterested.

Orion seems a little less so. "What's inside?"

We're relaxed, just like any family that meets on a Sunday morning, congregating in the shared living space, discussing the issues of the day.

"I remembered the other day, my father kept my school stuff and most of my drawings. But he also kept photos of me with my nannies."

Orion and Logan freeze at the same time. They put down their cups and turn to me with a clear renewed interest in what I'm about to say.

"...And I found a picture," I say after a pause.

"And you waited all this time to tell us?" There's a threat in Orion's dark voice.

"I wasn't sure, and I didn't wanna talk about her without being certain. I'm sorry." I look at Logan. "I spent all this time going through my father's old stuff, trying to find anything."

Logan crooks his eyebrow at me.

"And I have," I add, and pat the box in front of me. "I called every nanny 'Mom,' but her, I knew her name was Becca. She told me. She was different than the others. She was so loving. That's why I remember her. I remember her helping me get dressed. We painted silly faces. She never made me eat what I didn't like. And, she read to me. A lot."

I look at the box in my lap, old and slightly worn. I lift the lid and brace myself for the flood of memories. Orion and Logan lean closer, obviously desperate to see a glimpse of our mother. I start going through a few photographs of birthdays, and holidays, not only of me, but of all the kids I grew up with. We were one big, happy family. Until we all grew up, and learned what being in the mob really means.

I locate the photograph I've already seen and hold it up. "Here I am, age four. I didn't wanna wear my shoes that day, so she carried me in her arms all the way to kindergarten. Take a look. Our mother."

I hand the photograph over to Orion. Logan moves beside him and perches on his armrest. Both of them stare at the picture.

"Are you sure that's her?" Logan asks.

"It can't be anyone else. You have her features, Logan."

"I do?"

I nod, and resume sifting through the photographs.

"I found another one. Let me see... Clearly, it's Thanksgiving, there's the turkey on the table, and there she is. Holding a card. What does it say?" I squint, trying to read. "Does it... Does it say 'I'm sorry'?"

Orion snatches it from my hand and checks it himself.

"I kinda remember her saying that she wrote that by mistake or something, but that she was happy to take a photo with it," I add.

"Yeah, it says 'I'm sorry,'" Orion confirms.

"Do you think that's a message for us?" Logan asks. Maybe he's holding onto a sliver of hope, desperate for any evidence that she was thinking about us.

I come across a book that she read to me when I was little and my heart leaps. "Oh my god! I haven't seen this book in forever! It was my favorite!" I pull it out of the box. "She read it to me every single night. *The Three Little Wolves and the Big Bad Pig.*"

I pass it to Logan, who opens it and flips through the pages. "What kind of book is this? I remember the three little pigs, but not wolves?" he asks.

"Yeah, that's why I loved it, it was different," I say.

Logan turns back to the inside cover, then stops and stares at it. "This is a message from her. No doubt about it."

"I don't remember any message," I say. "I haven't seen this book since I was five."

"To Kai, may you find your wolfpack one day," Logan reads aloud as Orion peers over his shoulder.

"Fuck me," I mutter.

Orion leans back in his chair, and Logan comes back to the couch. The three of us must be thinking the same thing. She *did* leave us clues.

"Do you have any other photos of her?" Orion asks.

"Possibly, I just have to sift through more junk in my father's basement."

"Do that," Logan says, tracing her written words in the book with his finger.

"Look, each of these items is a memory of her, and if it makes you feel connected, I want you to have them," I say. "Either the photos or the book."

"And you?" Logan asks, sounding wary.

"I have my memories of her, Logan."

"Thanks, Kai. I want the Thanksgiving photo," Orion says.

I didn't expect him to want anything, but it's clear he's as affected by this as I am. He just hides it better. "I think Logan would appreciate holding on to the book," I suggest.

Logan nods. "Thanks, Kai. Her message did get through."

"Don't mention it," I say. "You know, if her family never got killed, I wonder if we'd have been born to her at some point when she got married, never to experience mafia life, or if we'd be born to whoever our fathers slept with, and never be brothers at all."

"What?" Logan frowns, trying to make sense of it while I laugh on the outside, but there's a lump forming in my throat. If we continue this conversation, I'm gonna start crying. And I don't do that.

Maisy shows up in all her glory, in a very tiny white top and a pair of white panties. "What's going on?"

"Kai's become a philosopher," Orion scoffs.

"What's all this?" She picks up the photo of the Thanksgiving dinner, and her eyes almost bulge out of her head. She looks at me, then at Orion, then Logan. "Your mother! That's her! Look!"

"You're sure it's her, right?" Logan asks.

"Yes! This one here, holding the card!" Maisy points to the face in the photo. "Where did you get these?"

"From my basement. Come, sit next to me, Maisy." I pat the space beside me on the couch. I set the old box on the coffee table and lean back, and she throws herself down on the seat, her boobs jiggling.

"Your boobs are big," I joke.

She immediately shoots back up to her feet. "If we're gonna talk about this, I'm going to my room." She's clearly not ready to talk about her body changing, or even the prospect of her being pregnant.

"What? Wait, I didn't mean it," I protest.

Orion leans forward. "Maisy, what's going on? What's happening with you?"

She doesn't leave; if she'd tried, he'd have grabbed her hand and pulled her back.

Instead, she shrugs, and her chin wobbles before she bursts into tears. "I don't know. Don't know anything. I cry and I laugh, and I feel so emotional, and I'm always tired... and..."

The three of us look at each other. We know what this is. But how come she doesn't?

"Well, for starters, we haven't used protection." Logan is in medical practitioner mode. "All these symptoms, changes of mood, being tired, eating more... Have you considered that you *might* be pregnant?"

She looks up at Logan and wipes at her tears. "You mean, the twenty pregnancy tests you kept leaving in my room were not enough of a clue?" A small smile begins to penetrate her sad expression.

Suddenly, she bursts out laughing, the sound mingling with her sobs. The laughter transforms her face and she seems lighter, the room itself seeming to brighten around her as she embraces this unexpected moment of joy.

I laugh, but I'm wary. Is she going crazy? What is all this? She was crying only a second ago. And look at her now, laughing like nothing happened.

I glance over at Orion and Logan and they laugh with her, too. But at the same time, I feel their eyes on me a tad too long, as if they're letting me in on something. *What's the damn secret?*

"You did lose your sister only a little while ago. That could be it," I say, but instantly regret it when she resumes wailing and weeping. I rake my fingers through my hair; I got no idea what I'm meant to do right now.

Logan sits beside her, drapes his arm around her shoulders, and lets her lean into him for support.

After ten long minutes of crying, she finally speaks. "I don't want to be pregnant. I don't want my child to have a life like mine."

"A life like yours?" Orion asks. "You mean, a life full of courage and bravery? Don't you ever undermine your life, Maisy. I won't allow it."

That makes her stop crying. She sniffles and dabs at her eyes. She looks at Orion, at me, and then at Logan.

"No one knows if you *are* pregnant," Logan says. "You're feeling like this because someone said something. You may not be pregnant at all. The body goes through changes once you get off the contraceptive implant. I'm sure you knew that already."

She thinks for a moment and nods. "Yeah. I did. You're right."

"Of course I'm right." He tucks a strand of hair behind her ear. "How about this. How about we take you out for dinner today, but before the restaurant, we're gonna stop by the hospital for a quick ultrasound. You don't have to take a pregnancy test if you don't want to. We'll do this instead. Is that okay?"

"Mm-hmm." She nods and wipes the remaining tears from her face.

CHAPTER 18

ORION

"Is this possible? Could she really be pregnant?" While we wait for Maisy to get ready to go to the restaurant – via the hospital, for the ultrasound – I consider every possibility.

Logan's pissed. "I don't know, Orion. I didn't know ten minutes ago and I don't know now. The fact that I'm a doctor doesn't give me magical powers. I follow the science, as everyone does, but she hasn't let us use it on her yet."

Jeez. No one forced him to be a doctor. He chose to be. Now he's gonna take it out on us, the commoners.

"But all this could easily be the side effects of the implant, right?" Kai asks.

Logan exhales frustratedly. "I wish you'd both stop with the questions. The moment Maisy comes out of her room, we're going. Why can't you be a little more patient?"

The evening can't come soon enough. The three of us have been ready for the past hour. And I'm done waiting. For the tenth time, I walk past the mirror opposite the elevator and check myself out. I'm in my usual black shoes, white shirt, and black three-piece suit. I'm clean-shaven and have tried to slick back my dark hair, but since it's wavy, it's fucking hard. I'm trying a different look I think, a mature one, if such a thing exists.

Basically, I'm being stupid. I'm nervous. That's what I am. I look over at Kai, and after observing him for a while, I realize he always looks better than the both of us, even though he steers away from suits. His black jeans, black shirt, and biker jacket look good with his messy blond locks. Logan's the calmest of all of us, a side effect of his profession, and also because he talks slow and measured, which makes everyone believe he's this laid-back guy. Which he isn't, as I know for a fact. The pockets of his pants are filled with blades, even now, when there's no need for them.

I know he's had enough of us asking questions. I've had enough of myself at this point. But I want to be fully in the know for Maisy's sake, and I want to know how to support her. Right now, I just feel like a fish thrown onto dry land.

My ridiculous thoughts disintegrate the moment I see Maisy walking down the corridor toward us. Fuck me. The woman in her has made an appearance. In her eyes, she holds a hundred kingdoms. She's truly made an effort, or maybe that's my dick talking because I didn't fuck her this morning. Whatever it is, I like the feeling.

Kai and Logan have had their heads turned too. *Good, so I'm not going crazy then.*

I think it's what she's wearing. She's ditched her usual jeans and shirt for a black pencil skirt, a white shirt, and a pair of black pumps. The top three buttons of her shirt are undone, her heavy breasts practically spilling out of it.

Her dark waves bounce as she walks, but then she stops mid-step and turns back to her room, and for a split second, I get a glimpse of her ripe buttocks swelling against the taut material of her skirt.

She appears to change her mind, spinning on her heel and coming back. Toward us.

She sucks her ring finger in her mouth as she walks, swinging her hips, and I've never seen her more beautiful. It's like, right in front of our eyes, she's grown. Our Maisy.

"See, see my finger? I managed to cut it while I was getting dressed," she says, approaching us and holding up the injured finger.

My eyes are drawn past her hand to her breasts. I adjust my cock, making more space in my pants.

"It's nothing. Let me take care of it, sweetheart." Logan kisses her finger, and doesn't stop there. *Asshole.*

"I don't think we have time for that, *doctor.*" If he thinks I'm gonna delay this ultrasound thing a moment more, he's mistaken. "Maisy?" I offer her my arm.

She grins, accepts it, and together we stroll along to the elevator, past Kai.

"So, we're going then?" Kai asks.

Logan puts his arm around his shoulder when he reaches him. "Delgado, I hope you're ready."

"Ready as I'll ever be," Kai mutters.

Emilio's already waiting for us outside. I know Logan wants to start using his car but I think we all trust Emilio, and Emilio only drives my car. And mine can fit the four of us in the back. Logan and Kai get in first, and I allow Maisy to enter by herself. The way she moves about in her tight skirt, giving us a glimpse of her thighs, *fuck*, my cock will be aching all night, I know it. She sits next to Kai and I sit opposite, next to Logan.

The three of us watch her as she leans back and tries to put her seatbelt on. She knows we're watching her. Her breasts are seriously too big for the shirt she has on. Why would she buy a shirt so small?

She's struggling with the buckle, and as much as I want to enjoy watching her breasts getting squished, I'm not that cruel.

"Maisy, leave it," I tell her.

"I can do it." But she can't. She's flustered.

"Since when do we use seatbelts, baby girl?" Kai places a hand on her thigh and instantly, she calms down. He takes the seatbelt from her hand and kisses her on the head.

For most of the drive, we ride in silence. Emilio probably senses that things are not right and after enough awkward silence, he turns the radio on.

"Which restaurant are you taking me to?" Maisy asks over the music. Her voice is sweeter than sugar. Soft. Like a mermaid calling sailors to their deaths, she's calling to my cock.

"Restaurant?" Logan frowns, looking like he's been caught off-guard. Probably because all he's thinking of is that ultrasound.

"Sushi Nakazawa in West Village," I tell her, prepared.

Maisy locks eyes with me briefly before turning to gaze out the window.

"But remember, we said we're first going–" Logan starts.

"I know," she interrupts, her gaze still fixed on the view through the glass.

~

"You know where we're going, Logan?"

We definitely won't be staying at the hospital for long; we're clearly out of place here, and people are staring at us.

"Sure I do. Just follow me."

Logan and Maisy walk next to each other, and Kai and I follow close behind.

We go through double doors marked *Obstetrics and Gynecology*, and straight on to the reception area, where two blond nurses sit. Logan quirks a smile at one of them and nods. In response, she gestures to the door to our left that reads *Sonography Room 2*.

Logan leads us into the room, and as the four of us enter, we startle the grey-haired doctor inside, who stands up in protest.

"Um, excuse me, please, could you wait for your tur–" the man starts, but Kai grabs him by the throat and squeezes.

Kai's hands are strong and I'm afraid he might do real damage. We didn't come to kill today. Besides, I told the Vitalis and Delgados already: never, ever do business where innocent passersby could get hurt. We learned that the hard way, and I'll be damned if something like that happens again.

And in any case, we don't intend to leave many dead bodies behind with our new way of working. As it worked out, Uncle Jon, Uncle Leo, and Tom get along so well, their proposal for our joint venture is turning out to be better than any of us imagined.

"What was that, old man?" Kai growls.

"Kai," I warn, signaling it's time to release him. As he does, the doctor breaks out in a coughing fit and I pat his back. "We're gonna be using this room for a short while, doc. I advise you to wait outside until we're done."

He nods, petrified, and hurries outside.

There's a bed next to the ultrasound machine, and Logan ushers Maisy to lie on it.

Logan immediately gets into the role of an OB/GYN. He sits on the chair in front of the machine and turns it on.

"Is this okay?" Maisy asks, propping herself up on a large pillow.

"Perfect. Just lie down, let me get this ready."

I move to the other side of the bed and sit on the edge, while Kai stands behind me. Together, we all stare at her. And I sense her withdrawing from us.

Kai, Logan, and I discussed this. It was a no at the time. But honestly, things changed. Not sure how, but they did. And look at her now, she's just... perfect.

I take her hand in mine, and immediately she squeezes back. She needs comfort and reassurance. This has been an anxiety-inducing time and I see it now – all she needs is my support. And I haven't given it to her. I've been stuck in my own head, thinking selfishly about this whole thing.

"Don't worry, darling, we got you," I say.

Her eyes are glossy. She's fighting back tears.

Logan takes over. "Hey, it's gonna be okay. I just want you to pull your skirt down a little, past your tummy, and hold your shirt up and out of the way." He helps her tuck her shirt up and pull the skirt down. "That's good. Now, I'm gonna put gel on your tummy. It's a little cold, so brace yourself."

He squeezes a few dollops onto her skin. Maisy shudders but says nothing.

"Turn the lights down, Kai, and let's... all... look... *here*."

I focus on the ultrasound screen, enhanced by the newly dimmed lights.

Logan moves the wand over Maisy's stomach, and the black-and-white image on the monitor begins to reveal shapes and forms.

I concentrate in silence, trying hard to make sense of the screen, but it's all unclear to me. After a moment, I glance at Logan. I notice that Maisy and Kai are also watching him, absorbed by his actions.

He stops, sucks in a breath, and runs his hand through the dark hair falling over his face.

"Rosey was wrong," Logan announces and looks at Maisy, his voice neutral. "I don't see a baby in here."

A mix of relief and unexpected disappointment immediately fills the room. It's strange. We all wanted this result, didn't we? Yet the air feels heavy, tinged with a peculiar sadness.

"Oh." Maisy bites her lip and looks up at Logan, who reaches for her hand, squeezing it tightly. She regards me, and then Kai. She's sharing a complex flood of emotions from the black universe of her eyes, gratitude mingled with a twinge of sorrow. I feel it too. I think, beneath my initial fear, there was a part of me that had started to imagine a different future.

"...I see *two* babies." Logan smiles and points out two small, distinct shapes. "Here's one," he says, and then pauses, moving the wand across Maisy's belly to show the other shape. "Here's number two. Twins!"

The screen displays the image of not one but two tiny, pulsing heartbeats. Maisy gasps.

Dumbfounded is exactly what I am. I have no words; I just exchange awkward glances with Kai, then with Maisy, and I end up on Logan, who's grinning. I'm surprised by the complexity of my feelings. Is it possible for one man to experience all that I am at this very moment?

The revelation shocks everyone. Maisy's eyes are wide with surprise. Kai's jaw drops open, and I just stare at the screen, speechless. The room is silent for a moment as the reality sinks in.

"Oh, wait, let me put the sound on." Logan rolls his eyes at his forgetfulness. As if he didn't just say Maisy is pregnant and she's carrying two babies. Two. *Two. TWO!*

Suddenly, the room fills with the rapid, rhythmic sounds of the twins' heartbeats.

Maisy's eyes grow even wider. I squeeze her hand gently as my heart races with anticipation. Kai moves closer to her and puts his hand on her shoulder as he watches the monitor.

Maisy's breath hitches in her throat. This whole moment is surreal. Tears well up in her eyes, but I don't see fear at all. All I see is a deep, visceral connection that is immediately evident, and a whole lot of wonder.

This woman faces challenges with the heart of a champion.

"Are-Are you all okay? 'Cause I'm fine, I really am. Don't worry, you won't have to do a thing," she babbles, like she's trying to fill the uncomfortable void we assholes have created with our silence. "I know I didn't want kids, but there's no way I'm not having *them.* I mean, look at them..." Her voice falters and tears begin to roll down her face as she points to the little shapes on the screen, two tiny lives. "They're so helpless, so small, and I'm gonna protect them," she whispers through her

sobs. "I'm gonna do everything for them. They're...
They're mine." She wraps her arms around her stomach,
as if we're gonna take them away from her at any
moment.

"Hey, *hey*, Maisy! Stop, just stop!" I grasp her
shoulders, pulling her back from her tearful daze. "We're
here, we're not going anywhere. There's not a force in
this world that would keep us away from you, in this life
or any other lives we may have. Remember that!"

"Orion," she sniffles, and swipes at the ever-
flowing tears on her face. "It's fine. It's okay. J-Just give
me a few weeks to find a place to stay."

"Maisy, I don't know what you're thinking, but
I'd walk to the end of the earth for you!" Kai insists when
she turns to him. "What makes you think we're not okay
about your... actually, *our* babies? In fact, I'd walk across
the globe on razors for our babies. Twice!" He gives a
forced chuckle, attempting to lighten the mood.

Maisy looks at the three of us with a lamenting
look in her eyes for a lingering moment, and sighs sadly.
That look just killed me. In her world, I didn't see myself
anymore. Or any of us.

"You got to let me go. I will never be able to love
you as much as I will love my babies, and... I will never
choose you. And it's okay. Really." The tears don't stop
falling from her eyes, but she doesn't seem to notice
anymore. "I'm not going to send Rosey's children to a

home. How could I?" Her voice fades to a whisper. "They belong with me. I owe that much to her." She tries to straighten her posture, put on a strong front, but it's futile. I can see her breaking apart in front of our eyes. I'm breaking apart on the inside. "I'm sorry, but I choose them over you. I... I guess you were right. I am a 'fucking Slav.' I betrayed you. I double-crossed you. If I wasn't pregnant, I'd ask you to kill me for doing this to you. Because that would be easier than what I'm going to go through." She continues to sob in earnest.

Logan cleans up the gel from her stomach and then wipes the tears from her cheeks. "Sweetheart, don't say things you don't mean."

"Logan, you were my protectors all this time, and I thank you for that," she says, "but now it's time for me to protect my babies. And I'm forever grateful to you for keeping me alive long enough for me to see the purpose of my life."

"A-Are you leaving us?" *She's made up her mind?* This is not real.

She looks at me and the tears overtake her once more. Her face contorts painfully with remorse. "Orion," she sniffles, "I promised Rosey I'd look after her four children. I'm also pregnant with twins. That's six children altogether. No one wants to look after six children. And I will never ask you to do that."

"*Ask* me? Are you crazy?" I bark at her. "You don't get to ask me to look after you! That's a given! You are part of us! Especially now that you're carrying our twins! And so fucking what if you're looking after your sister's children? Yes, they're Slavs. Yes, I hate the idea, and yes, I'm gonna have to get used to it, but fuck me if I'm gonna let you live anywhere else but with us!"

"Fuck yeah!" Kai roars.

"Sweetheart, did you really think you were gonna break up with us?" Logan asks.

Maisy's eyes are locked on Logan. Maybe because he's less intimidating than Kai and I are right now.

"You have to get it in your smart little head that we love you," he continues, "and we're here to stay."

I stand up. "I'm not gonna dwell on what you were trying to do just now, because if I do, I'll get mad again. Instead, I'll say this: Maisy Roy, congratulations! You have all the makings of a great mother!" I pull her into an embrace.

"The best mother in the world!" Kai joins the hug, and Logan does too, leaning across the bed.

"I cannot wait to meet our babies," Logan murmurs.

As if this was an invitation for her to resume crying, she completely lets loose and bawls in our arms, tears of both joy and relief.

I pull away and wipe her eyes. "Silly girl." I shake my head and turn to Kai, who's closest to me. "Kai, congratulations, you're gonna be a dad!" I embrace him wholeheartedly.

"Thanks, man. Same to you! You're gonna be a *great* dad!" he replies.

It's stupid, but those words really do something to me. A dad. *I'm gonna be a great dad.* I turn to Logan on the other side of the bed. "Logan."

He walks around it and we embrace each other.

Kai joins us again, too. "Congratulations."

"Before I forget, let me print out an image of the ultrasound before we leave." Logan hurries back to the machine and presses a few buttons, and an image comes out of the printer. He passes it to Maisy.

Maisy, still looking dazed, stares at the image for a while. Her eyes fill with a new sense of purpose and joy.

"Two babies." She sighs. "Twins. Like Rosey and me."

CHAPTER 19

MAISY

It's a sunny afternoon, and I've managed to get away from everyone for a couple of hours. I'm sitting on the wooden bench, tucked away cozily in a secluded corner of the garden.

I love this spot. My boys couldn't have chosen a better place for the bench.

I look around and see Emilio's car in the distance. He's the one who gave me a ride, in secret. Although I don't need to be particularly smart to know that he's in fact updating the others on every step I take. Which I get, given my condition. Meh. I like that, in a way. They've become stupidly protective ever since we learned I've been carrying their twins.

A beautiful butterfly flutters in front of me. I focus on the near distance, and its beauty sharpens in front of my eyes. I lift my hand, offering it a place to land. And astonishingly, it does. I gape at it in surprise, and dare not move. This is it. The wish I longed for so long to come true. I read something a long time ago, when I was a teenager: if a butterfly lands on you, it will represent rebirth, and renewal. A reminder that life is full of cycles and that you have the power to start afresh and embrace new beginnings. Just as the butterfly emerges from its cocoon, you too have the opportunity to leave behind old patterns and beliefs and embrace a new chapter in life.

This is what I wanted most of my life. Once I read that, I desperately tried to make it happen, until life took over. But look at this beauty now, telling me I'm ready to embrace the next chapter. I chuckle. Why did I need a butterfly to tell me that? I've been holding on for a speck of hope, giving in to superstitions, hoping life will magically get better. Only when I took things into my own hands did my life start to unravel. And it has unraveled for the worst at every step of the way, until now.

I pat my stomach gently and look around at the plot of land on which Milan's house stood, what was once the Slav headquarters. All this is now mine.

At first, I didn't know how to feel about it. This was a place where great atrocities were committed; people were tortured, raped, and killed here. My stomach churns when I think about what went on. Maybe even my father had a role in it. In fact, I'm sure he did. But as Rosey's next of kin, all this belongs to me now.

Orion paid someone to knock down everything that was still standing and clear the whole plot of any debris. Once they did that, the land was turned into a beautiful green lawn filled with wildflowers. That's when they put the bench in.

The back of the garden backs onto a park, and even though it's a great location, I'm still not sure what I'm going to do with it. But it sure is nice having something to my name.

The butterfly flutters away from me and after a short detour, it lands on the square memorial stone in front of me. I gaze at the stone, letting the memories flood back, feeling the weight of them in my heart. It's such a simple stone, with a clear inscription at the top: R.T. Underneath, my boys added more words, now sharply cut into the stone: *Rest in peace now. Your three wolves are looking after you.*

Here lies the remains of my boys' mother, and my twins' grandmother, Rebecca Trellis. I pat my stomach again as I think of the woman in that basement, and of her strength, her courage to try to amend her wrongs. She dedicated her entire life to vengeance, and yet love set her free.

Here I am, on land that I own, with babies in my womb, and three men who adore me. This never seemed possible in my world before.

From having no one for years, and living the life of an orphan, to having the biggest family anyone could ever wish for.

Orion, Logan, Kai, my twins, Maxim, Luca, Damien, and Mila. Lisa and Mia, too. From one to eleven family members in the course of a year.

That's all I wanted. A family.

I smile and look up at the cloudless sky. "Thank you, Rebecca. I got your wolves together. I hope you can see them. I'm also keeping them, if you don't mind. Someone's gotta look after them." I chuckle. "And please, please look after my babies. No matter what. They are the most important little humans in this world to me."

I feel her; I feel her presence. She's watching us, helping us.

I hope she won't mind us moving her remains when the time comes. Orion, Logan, and Kai couldn't decide which house we would live in, only because so much space is necessary for everyone, so now they're building a new house for all of us. One with a backyard. That's where we'll take Rebecca. To be with her family, every day.

To remind us that love always wins.

And vengeance eats you alive.

EPILOGUE

This was my first time watching Kai box. And I made an effort. I wore red and red only. Heels, halter neck minidress – on the tight side – panties, the whole nine yards. I wanted him to see me, to be proud of me. To win for me. Orion said the win was guaranteed, not because of anything illegal, but because this was the final and Kai knows what he's doing.

So maybe I shouldn't have come. I ruined the match for him. Actually, he ruined it himself, although in their world, I know there's a way around it. He is, after all, a mafia head. Everyone fears him. Everyone, except some young, inexperienced, and uninformed young man who, for the fun of it, wants to hit on the mother of Kai's children. Me.

I didn't want to come. Orion and Logan persuaded me. They insisted I leave my beautiful girls, Ava and Grace, with our babysitter and go out with them.

Apparently, the club is where all the fun is, and tonight they were particularly happy to bring me because they wanted to surprise their half-brother. He was going to win the championship belt for the streets.

He was gonna win a fight for me.

I'm not too keen on watching his face getting pummeled, so I tried not to look at him often and instead chat with Orion and Logan. Both of them look so smart every time we go out that it's hard not to look at them. Logan's hair is sleek, and Orion's wavy. And I felt like a million-dollar woman in my red dress with two tall, muscular, suited men accompanying me. Not only are they stupidly handsome, but they rule the city with their brains.

As a lawyer, Orion is slaying the district attorney's cases one by one. He even invited back every Slav who relocated with the help of the U.S. Marshal, Christopher – who, coincidentally, was outraged when the case against me collapsed because of lack of evidence. But I won't spare one thought about him.

As for Logan, he dons a white coat to go to work these days. A doctor. We need a doctor in the family, anyway. That spark from inside him, that compassion and empathy that shine through – no one could tell that he's a cold-blooded killer when he needs to be. At times it confuses me, because I know him and I see him for who he is. I was also there when he was being tortured, so I feel like I know Logan most intimately. After his torture, he could have become a ruthless asshole who didn't care about anything or anyone, and yet, he didn't. He is the sweetest man on earth. When he wants to be.

And Kai, Kai is incorrigible. He loves riding bikes, and boxing. Oh, and his new obsessions, Ava and Grace. He really is prepared to walk on razors for them. Which sounds a bit dramatic, but it's true nevertheless.

Usually, I wouldn't be persuaded to attend today, but if I'm honest, I succumbed to my desire; I wanted the three of them in one go.

The club was packed, the crowd was loud, and I sat between Orion and Logan, watching Kai on and off, hoping to avoid any messed-up hits he took, when I noticed someone watching me from the other side of the ring.

Everyone in there knew who my men are, who I belong to. Everyone.

Scratch that – apparently not everyone. This young cock dared to approach me and ask for my number. The fact that I was sitting between two men didn't stop him. Clearly, he's new. It's what they say: the man who fucks is not the smartest or handsomest, but the one who's most persistent.

In any case, Kai saw him, jumped out of the ring – forfeiting the match altogether – and started punching the poor guy. Orion and Logan joined in, and Emilio just pulled me out of the commotion and took me straight to the car.

And now I'm sitting in the backseat of our car, still reeling from the adrenaline. Emilio is at the wheel, and Orion, Logan, and Kai are here with me, each of them with a bloodied face and knuckles. Still, they're buzzing from the evening's events.

"The nerve!" Orion exclaims. "But did you see me? I gave him my best left hook!"

"What a fucking asshole!" Logan agrees. "He's lucky I didn't cut off his balls right there, in front of everyone!"

"Yeah, right. If I didn't jump in, you two would've been squashed by him," Kai smirks as he undoes his boxing gloves. He's still in his shorts – he didn't even wait to change.

"Yeah? You want some? Come and get it!" Orion nudges Kai, and I immediately separate them.

"Hey, hey, stop being kids!" I laugh. This evening, no matter how short it was, was great. I dressed up, which means I felt good about myself, and now I get to take the three of them home.

The mood in the car shifts from one of excitement to one of anticipation. I think it's on all of our minds what's to come, but if and only if the children are asleep. Most likely they won't be. But we're hopeful.

Emilio navigates the streets with ease, a route he's driven many times before, only occasionally glancing at us in the rearview mirror whenever our laughter grows extra loud.

When we finally pull up to the house, I thank Emilio as always, and he offers a slight nod and a smile.

Our house ended up bigger than I could've imagined. Than any of us imagined. We kept amending the initial plans. And I can't get enough of the end result. I love the fact that the front door opens into a spacious open-plan area where the living room and kitchen blend seamlessly into one another. Despite its size, the living room feels cozy, with a couple of large couches and a fireplace. The kitchen is modern, with a huge island in the middle and high-tech appliances that I love using.

The moment we enter, Orion, Kai, and Logan's rowdiness is immediately subdued, and the stark contrast to the outside noise is felt.

The babysitter, Sasha, is on a couch in the living room with a book open in her lap. "You're back early," she says.

"Where are the kids?" Orion eyes the other empty couch, since they sometimes fall asleep on it.

She smiles. "Fast asleep in bed."

I raise my eyebrows at her, surprised. "All of the children?" She has babysat before, but she always had help. My children are a handful. And all of them under the age of six.

"Yes."

"Maxim?"

"He didn't put his pajamas on, but he's asleep."

"Luca?"

"He didn't brush his teeth, and he fell asleep on the couch, so I had to carry him upstairs. But he's asleep."

"Mila?"

"You mean the fussiest eater I've ever seen? She was an angel. Fast asleep."

"Damien?"

"You know Damien, he's as sweet as pie. Fast asleep. I gave him his bottle and he went to bed on his own. Seriously, I don't know what they did today, but all of them were truly tired."

"Told you, that trip to the zoo did the trick." Logan grins. "We encouraged them to walk most of the time."

"Well, they were so tired, they barely ate their dinner." Sasha laughs. "Ava and Gracie were last to fall asleep, maybe a half hour ago. They had their bottle of milk, so they'll be fine for the next four hours. Here's the baby monitor." She passes me the little gadget showing five interchanging screens, one for each of the kids' rooms.

Sasha babysits for us often; she has the patience of a saint, she's dependable and kind, and the kids love her, so we love her. Plus her father belongs to the Vitali family, so she knows how things work around here.

I walk over to the side table where my purse is and pull out a hundred-dollar bill. "Thank you."

She grins. I don't blame her. I only wish I was given hundred-dollar bills when I babysat when I was young.

"Come on, I'll get Emilio to drive you home," Logan offers.

She gathers her things as Logan shows her to the door.

"Get home safe," Orion calls out.

I leave Kai and Orion standing in the living room as I walk to the kitchen. I didn't get to have anything to drink at the club.

"I need a drink," Kai declares. His bloodied face looks better than any other day I've seen him after a match. Maybe because the fight didn't last long at all. He heads to the counter.

"I'll get it." I open the cupboard and take out four glasses and the bottle, and start pouring.

"Darling, I want you sober." Orion's voice is deeper, and darker. It catches me off-guard, and I need a moment before I reply.

"Why is that?" I reply as nonchalantly as I can as he slowly approaches me, but I already have butterflies fluttering around in my belly. God, it's been a while. I place the bottle on the counter and pick up my glass. Kai's watching me now too.

"You tell me," Orion says.

He's standing behind me and I remain still, deliberating over whether I should drink the whiskey. I think it serves me right for falling asleep on them the last time we wanted to play. I only had one glass of wine. But I was so tired. Would the whiskey knock me out too, I wonder?

Placing his hands on my shoulders, he starts massaging me gently, and I close my eyes, totally surrendering to the moment. I set the whiskey back on the counter, not because of what he said, but because it would have fallen out of my hand. I moan quietly. This is pure heaven.

"Do you want me to massage you?"

His hands slide down my body, tracing my curves. Then he reaches for the hem of my dress and starts gently tugging it up. His palms, now gliding up my body, feel warm and smooth on my skin.

He nips my ear and whispers, "Or do you want me to make love to you?"

It's been a while since we played. I don't remember the last time their hands were on me. My baby brain's forgotten everything. Wanton, and impatient, I turn around in search of his lips; I want him, and I want whatever he has planned for me. I want that debauched promise in his eyes.

He grins at my frustration and continues dragging my dress north with his hands, and upon reaching my chest, his thumbs search out my nipples, spinning a carnal need into my head. I stopped breastfeeding the girls a few months ago and it's been a while since my men enjoyed them properly.

Impatient, I lift my arms and allow the dress to be lifted over my head and dropped to the floor.

Logan's back now, sipping his whiskey and watching my every move like a hawk. As is Kai. As for Orion, his eyes never leave mine, even though I'm standing naked in front of him bar my red panties and red heels. He takes a step back and shucks off his suit jacket and tie, partially unbuttons his shirt, then rolls up his sleeves. The lean, perfect ridges of the muscles on his forearms are suddenly what I'm focused on, together with the rings on his fingers and the watch. And those damn bracelets... He looks so sexy.

"Kiss me," I beg, but he just runs his thumb over my lips, glides it across, slowly wetting it with my saliva and then inserting it into my mouth. My arousal surges, my insides are on fire; my body is in charge now and it walks the path that he's crafting. How he does it, I cannot comprehend.

He takes his thumb out of my mouth. "What's it gonna be, Maisy?"

"Make love to me, Orion," I whisper, my throat thick with anticipation.

He glides his wet thumb down and over my left breast, softly touching my skin but deliberately skipping past my pebbled nipple. He does the same with my right breast and by now, fuck, my back is arched so hard it hurts.

Fuck this. In my head I'm thinking of twenty things at the same time, and I can't take this anymore; I take his hand and guide it to my breast.

"Touch me." I take his other hand and place it on my other breast. "Don't you want me?"

"Too much."

"Then why—"

"What's the rush, Maisy?" he whispers.

With his hands on my breasts, he starts kneading them gently; my hardened nipples rub against his palms, but they need more. I close my eyes and tilt my head sideways, extending my neck, hoping he'll get the message. I smile when I feel his lips on my skin. Each little kiss feels like he strikes a match, causing it to spark and flame. I'm slowly drowning when I feel his fingers tangling in my hair and pulling my head toward him. I open my eyes again and when they meet his, I receive a sharp slap across my breast, followed by a tug, rousing me to sudden heights that are unknown to me. I clench my teeth and moan.

I'm not sure what just happened, but the flash burn inside my body is something I want more of.

There's another slap across my other breast, followed by a long tug that makes me lose my mind even more.

"Hi," he says darkly.

Everything slows down again. He hovers over my lips, waiting for me to part them, and when I do, he presses his against mine, delivering a slow, deliberate kiss.

He holds my body with his kiss, and guides me backward toward the dining room, a separate room with a long table that seats twelve people, surrounded by chic chairs. I'm reminded that I'm down to my panties and heels, while he's barely lost any of his clothing yet. In one hand, he continues to cup my breast and knead it tenderly. Then he squeezes my nipple again, and tugs it until I moan in pain before he lets go.

I feel as if he's fucking me already, but he's only just touched me. I think I'm that desperate.

Having stopped at the table, he pushes some chairs away to gain access to it.

Then, he takes my hand and orders, "Lie down."

I lie on my back on the table as he positions himself between my legs, and after adjusting his enormous bulge, he lifts them and places my heels on the edge of the table.

Immediately, he starts shimmying my panties off. But instead of casting them aside, he brings them to his face and inhales my scent so deeply, it almost makes me die from embarrassment. Fuck, how long has it been?

I inhale sharply, overwhelmed. "Y-You didn't have to do that."

"How could I not? You drive me crazy, darling."

Having collected the bottle of whiskey and the glasses, Logan and Kai come in. Orion's glass is placed next to me on the table.

"Right on time," Orion smirks, then downs his drink in one, slams the glass back on the table, and slides it away from me.

I watch him go down between my legs, probably to see me trembling – did I mention it's been a while?! I close my eyes, fully surrendering to the moment. I need this.

He hooks his hands under my thighs to spread them open, and after blowing on my pussy, he comes up.

"You are one horny girl, Maisy, aren't you?"

I blink, and watch him admiring me, but I'm lost already, spread open like this. I'm hoping his face is going to find its way between my thighs, but instead, he quickly slaps my inner thigh, making me shudder. I regard him half with lust, half with shock when he smacks my other inner thigh, and then he startles me by pinching my folds together. Laughing darkly, he watches me writhing in a confused daze. I seek assurance from his black eyes, but they only draw me deeper inside his hedonistic world. His hand feels hot against my pussy but I need more, I need friction. A fucking lot more friction.

"Yeah, she is." I barely hear Logan's words; I'm so wound up in the sudden influx of desperation for Orion's tongue. I moan in discontent.

"Do you think you can come for me, like this?" he asks me, feeling like he's far away, but he must be close because his hand is holding my pussy closed and I don't like it one bit.

Without a second more of waiting, I press my palms against the table for leverage and start rolling my hips upward against his hand, as hard as I can. It's not long before my arousal seeps through; my pussy is becoming too slippery for him to hold and I use that, I'll use anything to get him to let go, or to hold still until I get where I need to get, if only for a brief moment.

"Orion, I can't anymore," I breathe. "Please, fuck me."

"I'm happy to step in, brother," Kai says.

I catch a glimpse of the deadly look Orion throws Kai, the one that says no one gets her before I do. Orion is the protector, but when it comes to me, he's the most selfish man I've ever known. I can't say that I don't like it. Suits me full well. Like now, when I'm hanging on to the edge of life, he's always there to help me fly.

Without being able to hold me any longer, he releases me and unzips his pants, his cock jutting out eagerly as I pull him closer by wrapping my legs around his body.

Without wasting a moment, his cock quickly rubs up and down my slit, allowing me to adjust to the coolness of his metal piercing right before he slams inside me. What tips me over the edge is his grunt; it sounds like he's going through a personal redemption while I'm being sent to heaven. A cry escapes my lips at the same time and I'm flying too, my body going through an awakening of its own kind. He pulls out and holds still, while I go crazy with need, and with my eyes barely open I immerse myself in his bottomless black pupils, ready to enter his world and never go back.

"There's my little slut. Welcome back, beautiful!" He grins and starts pounding into me, hard and fast. He holds my legs for leverage and each thrust is rough, and ruthless. I try, but I can't hold off much longer. I'm there, on the edge of revelation, when the waves tip me over and suddenly I'm in heaven, and a whole vibrant energy zings through me. My legs shake as he releases a loud, guttural groan. His seed comes forth at the same time as my cum gushes down his cock.

"Orion… Ohh-Ryon!" I pant as I orgasm.

"Fuck, Maisy, I don't think I can hold on much longer. You're so sexy," Logan breathes.

He's standing beyond my head at the other end of the table. I reach behind me to curl my fingers around his cock and pump him a few times. It's taut, veiny, and ready for me.

"Come closer, and open wide for the doctor, Maisy."

I show him my tongue as he helps me slide up a little, enough for my head to hang back over the edge of the table, and he doesn't wait. "Theeere you go…mmhmmmm…" He leans over me and starts pumping, throat-deep, each time groaning in pleasure.

Almost immediately, I sense someone tugging my nipples, taking me into another world; I arch my back to press into their hands. I want more of it.

They suck and bite my hardened nipples between their teeth, one then the other, building an ever-growing and burning desire between my legs. It has to be Kai.

"I hope you're ready for me, baby girl."

I can only reply with a muffled sound as Logan fucks my mouth. "Mm-hmm."

"For what I have for you, you're gonna have to turn around," Kai adds.

"Fuck you, Kai! Fuuuck..." Logan is not stopping. I don't care; let them decide what they are to do to me.

"Come on, she can still suck you off, let her turn," Kai says, and after a moment of being ignored, he grows insistent. "Fuck, man, I need her just like you do."

Logan pulls out with a groan, freeing my throat. I take a desperate breath. I didn't realize I was close to getting asphyxiated. Kai guides me to roll over onto my knees, and as I'm positioned as he wants, I feel his hands on my butt cheeks, parting them. I want to look back and see what's happening, but Logan's waiting on me, impatiently stroking his cock.

"Head down," Logan orders. I obey and he turns my head sideways, my cheek pressed to the table. "Open for the doctor."

I stick my tongue out; I know how he wants it, and I take him in. I love the fact that he's fully dressed, and only his cock is exposed whenever it's not fucking my mouth.

Orion fills their glasses with whiskey and hands them around. "To Maisy! May she live forever!" he cheers. Kai and Logan clink their glasses, down them, and slam them on the table.

I haven't even considered what Kai will do to me because I'm losing myself in the face-fucking from Logan. But then, with my ass up in the air, I feel Kai's tongue flit over my… my… my… Fuck, that's not my…

He holds my cheeks open as he explores, and I become instant putty in his hands because I've never experienced what he's doing to me right now. I even help him out by raising my bottom slightly.

"That's my girl." His distorted words only just break through my already scrambled consciousness.

I'd do anything to assist him. I lift my bottom even higher, roll my hips left and right, and then try to move up and down. Helping him devour me as much as he wants to. His fingers slide through my arousal and that's the end of me. I free myself from Logan's cock to moan.

"Kai! Yes! YES!" I'm toppled over with yet another sacred orgasmic surge ripping through my body, new sensations that before were inconceivable to me making me oblivious of the noises I make and the air humping I do. This debauched act is something new…

something so fucked up that I'm ready to be enslaved for the rest of my life to receive this over and over.

"Scream for me, baby girl! Tell me how much you want this!"

A long wail is ripped from my throat. Every single nerve ending in me is responding to his tongue and his fingers fucking me at lightning speed.

"Fuck, sweetheart, I'm cumming!" Logan pants in anticipation of his high.

In a daze, I grab Logan's cock and milk it, the wicked vibrations reverberating through my body and awakening a demon inside me, and all I want to do is fuck, and orgasm, over and over.

His first rope of jizz lands on my face and I make sure the rest hits my tongue, just the way he likes it.

"Oh yes, oh yes, oh yes!" he growls as he holds my head. I need oxygen, I think I'm gonna faint. I begin to float through space, and when I land, my cheek is still flat on the table. I pant, trying to catch my breath, completely out of my mind.

From the corner of my eye, I see Kai climbing onto the table, one knee down and one raised, his foot firmly planted for leverage. His fingers dig into my ass cheeks as he rams his cock into me. More waves wash over me, leaving me soaking wet, and I whimper now, loud. Really loud.

"You can do it one more time, Maisy. Show me, let me see you cum, baby girl," Kai commands.

I look back at him, and our eyes meet. His chest is glistening with sweat, his blond locks fall over his face, and his groans come with each thrust he makes. I'm flying high. And then he slaps me, right there on my ass cheek. Every nerve I possess is on edge and now more zings dart under my skin. How is it possible?

He reaches below and starts rubbing my swollen clit as he thrusts hard inside me. My legs begin to shake. Another slap on my ass stings me and reduces me to more whimpers, long and loud. It's upon me, I feel it. The moment he slides two fingers in my ass, I can't hear him any longer. I feel one more slap and that's it; I begin to erupt so hard that my whole body is convulsing, but he keeps pounding me until I'm moaning and gasping and shaking violently.

His growls get louder and his thrusts rougher before he stills inside me with a deafening groan.

We lie stuck to each other for a few moments while we return safely to earth.

"I can never get enough of you, my temptress," Kai whispers in my ear.

"Temptress?" I pant. I'm sated, and ruined. And yet, I want more of them.

I glance over at Orion and Logan. They're watching me predatorily as they finish their whiskey.

More? I can take more. Anything for my men.

295

The End

Thank you for reading KAI Tortured, the last book (Book 3) of the New York Mafia Vengeance series.

If you enjoyed the story please share the love, leave a review and / or recommend the series to your friends.

Thank you kindly!

298

ABOUT THE AUTHOR

Alexandra loves writing love stories, drinking Champagne and of course, wearing high heels.

Most days she is glued to her trusty laptop, creating magic, but on an odd occasion you'd find her on her social media accounts, connecting with her readers. Feel free to (virtually) follow her.

www.alexandraiff.com/links

Copyright

New York Mafia Vengeance Series

ORION Ruined

LOGAN Punished

KAI Tortured

ISBN:

Imprint: Manor House Press

Copyright © 2024 by Alexandra Iff